**THANK YOU** so much for buying this book!

As a way of showing gratitude, I wanted to extend a very special offer to you. I'm giving selected readers access to my **VIP Mailing List**. As part of this group, you will receive notifications about promotions and new releases!

Do you want to read more romance stories full of **Adventures**, **Passion,** and **Emotions** every week?

Go to http://eepurl.com/cMCM_D to join today!

# Thunder

## Savage Brotherhood MC: Book Three

## A Paranormal Romance

By Jasmine Wylder

# Chapter One

*Melanie*

If coffee came in a needle, Melanie would be tempted to shoot it directly into her veins. She slumped at her dressing station, resting her head in her hands, as she considered how long it had been since she had sat down. Her old, well-worn, strappy high-heels didn't hurt as much as her new pair would have, but not for the first time, she wished that she could just dance barefoot.

Ten hours at the cafe followed by ten hours at the club. The only thing keeping Melanie from quitting both her jobs that instant was the desire to someday leave this armpit of a town—and the fear of getting another bill from the hospital ranging into the thousands.

"Hey there, pussy-cat." The owner of the Chubby Kitty, the strip club which she danced at four nights a week, came up behind her and put a hand on her shoulder. It would have been an innocent enough touch, if it wasn't for the fact that no touch was innocent when it came to Rodger. "You were looking dead tired out there tonight."

Melanie dipped her shoulder so his hand fell off. "Yeah, well, it's been twenty-four hours since I was home, so I'm going to be tired."

Rodger pulled a sympathetic expression, as though he was actually concerned for her. He hadn't paid any attention to her, other than the usual leers, until his old favorite, Chrissy, abruptly quit. That was after he fed her tainted drugs that nearly killed her. Melanie wished she had that luxury. It wasn't so much the dancing or taking off her clothes that bothered her — it was the condescending looks, the sneers, the superior gleam in men's eyes when she did so.

Unfortunately, she needed the money. If she was ever going to get herself and her father out of Coalfell, then she needed to save enough to get a start in a new town. God knew that she couldn't rely on selling the house they lived in now. Its value would hardly cover the mortgage she'd had to take out to cover her father's medical bills when he first got sick.

"You have too much on your shoulders." Rodger sighed as he placed both his hands on her shoulders. His thumbs ran in circles, making her cringe. "You know, I know a few ways to help you relax."

What in the name of all that was holy had she done to deserve this? Had he found out that it was her who told Sheriff Cunningham that he was selling drugs to the girls? Not that it made much of a difference. Melanie pulled herself out of Rodger's grasp and gave him the most chilling smile she could muster.

"Maybe later. I have to go pick up some tampons."

He snatched his hands back so fast she might as well have put a gun in his face. His nose wrinkled in disgust. "Fuck. I don't need to know that." He stepped back, eyes narrowing. "Wear black underwear for the show tomorrow night."

She rolled her eyes. "I didn't wear black underwear tonight. I know how to keep the clients from seeing my bloody lady parts."

Rodger growled this time, looking sick. Melanie repressed a triumphant grin as she quickly shucked off her robe and wiped the sweat from her body. She ignored Rodger's look—she'd learned to deal with him and his stink long ago. He went after the most vulnerable girls and always mistook her as one of them. Yeah, she'd be screwed if she quit—but she'd find a way out of it.

After dressing, Melanie left out the back. The air was thick and heavy with rain, but after the oppressing air of the club, she had to stop and pull in a few deep breaths. Her cat purred, happy to finally be out of there.

The Chubby Kitty was named quite literally, though most of the clientele wouldn't know that. Every girl that worked there was a feline shifter. Most were fairly exotic, like jaguars or pumas. Melanie herself was what she deemed a 'feral cat'. In her animal form, she was hardly different from the strays that would sometimes hang out around the dumpsters. Her coat was long and fluffy, giving her an appearance similar to a Norwegian Forest Cat, but the truth of the matter was that she was nothing special. Too round-figured to get a job at a normal strip club. So, she was here, working her plus-size self in front of a bunch of chubby chasers.

Voices came from down the alley and Melanie tensed. Her hand went to her pocket, where she kept a small knife on her at all times. The club's clients were infamous for trying to convince the girls that they ought to do some private entertaining. As she headed for the parking lot, though, a smallish man suddenly barreled past her. She leapt back, jumping back into the entrance of the club.

A bear and a wolf shot across the doorway and pounced on the man. He screamed, an inhuman screech, as the bear clamped his head in its jaws and the wolf leapt for his throat. Melanie's scream caught in her lungs as the two tore the man apart.

The sickly-sweet scent of rotten fruit filled her nostrils along with the copper of blood. The bear's form rippled, shifting into a man's form. He hefted the dead man's corpse into the nearby garbage bin, while his companion slapped him on the back and laughed.

“That’s the fourth this week. When will they le—” The wolf shifter’s eyes widened when he saw her there.

“What’s—” The bear turned. His jaw dropped at the sight of her, as well.

Melanie bolted. Both men lunged at her. Without a thought, she shifted into her cat form. Her clothes melted off her. The men shouted in surprise, pulling up short as she darted between them. A fence blocked off the alleyway from the parking lot and she slipped underneath it.

There was a roar and a crash behind her. She didn’t need to look to know that the bear and wolf had broken through the fence. Heavy footsteps followed after her. Her fur stood on end as she pushed herself harder.

The wolf barked, sounding closer than she would have liked, and she zagged to the left. Teeth snapped shut, pinching the hairs on the end of her tail. She whipped around, throwing herself into the wolf's face. Claws raked down his face while she bit at his eyes. The wolf yipped, skidded to a stop and shook his head wildly. Melanie bit through one of his ears before she sprang away, this time darting under the bear's belly as he joined them.

She spied a drainage tunnel and darted into it. If she kept herself crouched down, it was just big enough to hold her. Too small for either of the other shifters. She settled down in the center, well out of reach from either side. Her chest heaved, and her heart pounded. The tunnel smelled of rotten things that were sure to stink up her fur. If she got out of here alive.

The wolf's face appeared at one side of the tunnel blocking out the sun. The bear came at the other side.

"Hey there," the wolf rumbled, panting. "That's quite the chase you set us on. Why don't you come out and let us talk, sugar? See, you saw a little misunderstanding and we just need to talk it out. Come on out, kitty. We're not going to hurt you, wolf's honor."

"What are you talking about?" the bear snarled. "She saw what we did! We can't let her go running around and blabbing. You want Blizzard to arrest us? Or worse... Shadow's going to kill us if she knows we took out a target in front of a witness. But not if we don't have a witness."

The wolf propped himself on his knees, hissing. “You idiot! How are we supposed to get her out of there if she thinks we’re going to kill her? What the fuck is wrong with your head?”

“What’s wrong with yours?” the bear shot back. “We can’t just let her go!”

Melanie shrank smaller in the center of the drainage tunnel. Her mind whirled to a thousand thoughts per second. Could she dart out while they were distracted, or would she just end up in their hands? If she was killed in this form, she would stay in this form. Nobody looked twice at feral cats on the side of the road. She’d be hauled off by the sanitation department. What would happen to her dad?

If she tried to shift in here, the pressure of the enclosed space would crush her. She'd end up dead. Perhaps never found—what would happen to her dad?

She couldn't see any way out of this... what was her father going to do without her?

"Idiot," the wolf growled. "Don't you know who that is? It's Ava's best friend. Mary or something like that. Do you know what Tornado would do to us if he found out we hurt his mate's best friend? We'd be better off skinning our own damn selves and staking our pelts to the wall."

"Fuck," the bear said, sounding surprised. "What the hell are we supposed to do, then?"

"Hell if I know! That's why we need to get her out, so we can talk. Maybe she'll be reasonable."

The bear crouched down again and peered in at her. "If I got a stick, I could poke her over to your side and—"

"Hell no! Did you see what she did to my face already?"

"Improved it, looks like," the bear chuckled.

His face disappeared again. Melanie laid her ears flat against her skull, beginning to creep that way. The bear seemed to be a real idiot, she might be able to slip past him and get away. The voices were more muffled now. The way the bear was kneeling, his naked crotch was right at the exit of the tunnel. If she had to, she'd take a swipe at it—

that ought to put him out of commission.

When she got to the end of the tunnel, she glanced back to make sure the wolf wasn't watching, then sprang forward.

The bear let out a shout as she flew out of the tunnel. Claws unsheathed, she made to attack. Something heavy slammed into her back. A fist grasped her at the back of the neck and yanked her into the air. Her skin went tight around her throat as the bear lifted her by her scruff. She growled in her throat, trying to make her legs kick and scratch. It was useless as the pressure on her scruff increased, forcing her body into shut-down mode.

"Got her!" the bear shouted triumphantly. "Hurry, if we wrap her up in your jacket she can't claw your face off again."

"Good thinking, genius, only I left my jacket at the car. Shit. We need to get back there before someone calls Blizzard down on us for being naked in public again. You'll just have to carry her like that."

The bear crossed the road in a few quick strides, grunting as he did so. He swung Melanie so much, she thought he might end up snapping her neck by accident. The two shifters hurried back the way they had come, half-hunched now to hide their nakedness.

"I don't like this," the bear grumbled, glaring at her. "What if she shifts and gets away?"

The wolf growled, but it was too late. Melanie had already shifted. The grip on her scruff became a hand on her neck. She stomped on the bear's foot while elbowing him in the gut. He released her, leaning over with a twisted expression. Melanie struck at the wolf, but he caught her by the wrist and pulled her off balance. Something hard knocked her in the head and everything went black.

***

The world was still black when she woke, her head throbbing. She lay on something scratchy and there were walls pressing in on every side. Something lay over her, a blanket, she thought, but she was naked beneath it. The space was hot and stuffy, and she was curled up into a fetal position.

Panic started to crawl up her throat, so she shifted. The space became much less confining once she was in her cat form. She purred to reassure herself that she was fine, trying to force herself to be calm. It didn't help. In her cat form, though, she saw that it wasn't entirely black in here. Thin strips of light came in a blocky pattern, allowing her to take a better look at her cage. The smell of gasoline and old shoes assaulted her.

A car trunk. She was in a car trunk. Well, thank God she hadn't suffocated! She licked her lips as she padded to the back of the trunk. They weren't moving and there were no voices around, which meant she might be alone here. If she could find the emergency release, then she could let herself out and be out of here before that bear and wolf knew what had happened.

Relief washed over her when she found it. She had been afraid that it would end up being an older model that didn't have one. Just as she maneuvered herself back into human form while maintaining a position she could open the trunk from, it suddenly opened.

Light stabbed her eyes, making them water. Melanie flinched back, a hiss on her lips. She let her nails turn to claws, ready to savage whatever gangster tried to make his move. When her vision cleared, and she saw the man looking down at her, she froze.

Fury radiated off him like a wildfire. His dark eyes narrowed and the hairs on her arms stood up. His lips pulled back in a half-snarl. He was shirtless, though he wore a leather jacket. A long scar ran from one shoulder to the opposite hip. The scent of wolf, wild, dangerous, rolled off him.

But that wasn't why she froze. He was the most handsome man she had ever seen. Tanned skin, chiseled abs, a strong jaw and a high forehead. Thick, dark hair. Her cat purred at the sight of him, batting paws against her ribs.

What the hell? Did her cat think this was a game?

Melanie shifted, leaping out of the trunk. The man grabbed at her and she swiped her claws over his muscled forearm, but he caught her without any difficulty. She twisted and snarled, biting and scratching his arms. He flung her back into the trunk and seized her by the back of the neck. He held her down, growling.

Her cat arched its back, telling her to stick her rear into the air as an offer. She hissed in annoyance at it. Here she was, liable to get her neck snapped, and it wanted to throw away her virginity on the gangster who was going to kill her? She hadn't saved herself all these years to get caught up with some selfish son of a bitch—not to mention that he was probably going to kill her now!

"You could have told me she was a shifter," the man growled. His voice was deeper than either of the other's, more authoritative. "Just what the hell do you expect me to do with her?"

# Chapter Two

*Thunder*

Zane pulled the cat from the car and held her away from him, one hand gripping her scruff tightly while using the other to support her so he didn't accidentally choke her. He glared at her, though he was angrier with the idiots from the Coalfell chapter than he was her. It was a wonder she hadn't suffocated in the trunk during the couple hours it took them to get here to Ivywood.

"Stop fighting me, sweetheart," he ordered, infusing his voice with the authority of the alpha he was. "Nobody's gonna touch you here."

The cat's green eyes bulged slightly. She let out a yowl and attempted a stiff swipe at his wrist. Zane rolled his eyes, released the hand holding her weight, and shrugged his jacket off that arm. He wrapped her tightly in it before he freed his other arm and held her to his chest. He could feel her heart pounding as he jerked his head at the two clowns from Coalfell and marched into the warehouse they'd come to. Several of his men gave them curious glances, but he ignored them and headed for his office.

Once inside, he shut the door and set the cat down on a chair.

"Feel free to shift back to your human form." One of the Coalfell idiots had brought the blanket, and Zane took it and laid it over the cat. "For your modesty."

The cat glared at him for a moment before she slowly shifted, clinging to the blanket around her body. “What are you going to do with me?”

The bear tapped Zane’s shoulder. “She’s best friends with Tornado’s mate.”

Zane gave him a glare that had him slinking back. “Are you telling me that you kidnapped your alpha’s mate’s best friend?”

The wolf shifted a little closer to the door. “She saw us taking out a target. We weren’t going to kill Ava’s best friend. But you’re the alpha of Ivywood, Tornado won’t go after you for taking care of her.”

It took a great deal of self-control not to turn and rip out the idiot’s throat. Because they were afraid of what Tornado would do, they had decided to bring her over here for someone else to kill? The cat whimpered, pulling the blanket higher over her chest. Zane spared her a moment to frown at her, noting the terror in her face, before turning back to the others. His wolf paced and snarled in his chest, eager to make them see that he wasn't some garbage disposal.

They were meant to protect civilians from vampires, not kill them. Unfortunately, she had seen too much. If she knew about vampires, then this wouldn't be such a dramatic situation. No. He couldn't let her go. He wasn't going to tell Tornado about it, either. Not since he'd become so soft for his mate. Zane shook his head—Tornado would probably just let her go running off to the authorities to spare his mate any distress.

"Get out of here," he growled at the two from Coalfell. "Before I give you cement shoes."

The two gulped and fled from the office, fighting each other to get out first. Zane glared after them before turning back to the woman. She stared at him warily. Brown hair tousled around her face, where makeup was smeared. There was a faint sweet odor about her, but the smell of feline was almost overpowering. It wasn't the same wild scent that he was used to with shifters, though. It was something more... controlled, almost.

"Well, this is a problem. What's your name?"

She stared at him, her jaw shut. There came a look of defiance in her eyes and she lifted her chin slightly.

"I'm not going to hurt you. For one thing, Shadow would tear off my balls if I did. I know you... you got mixed up in that drug stuff a few months back. Shadow has adopted you, and anybody who hurts her family gets torn to shreds."

Zane shook his head, the amusement at thinking of Tornado's younger sister abruptly cut short. Shadow, if rumors were true, was backing away from the gang. She'd mated with that traitor-cop Blizzard. What the hell was she thinking? Zane had thought there was chemistry between them, but clearly, he was wrong.

That didn't resolve what he was going to do with this pretty kitty, though. He sat on his desk, observing her in her continued silence. A streak of glitter ran over her cheekbones, highlighting them. She was very attractive. Her green eyes shone like fractures of gems, her skin smooth and clear. Lips were a little too large, but that just made them more kissable. With her hair tousled like that and the blanket clinging to her curvy frame, it made his wolf growl with pleasure. He'd like to get to know her in the biblical sense.

If his mother could hear his thoughts as he looked at this woman, who was clearly terrified just being in the same room as him, she would wring his neck.

"Did either of those idiots hurt you?" He made his voice gentle. "Did they..." How could he put this delicately? "Molest you?"

The cat shivered but shook her head. She swallowed hard. "I don't want to get involved in all this gang stuff. I just want to go home."

"I'm not in the habit of killing people who have done nothing wrong but be in the wrong place at the wrong time." He frowned, considering her as he cocked his head to one side. "Tell me what you saw."

"Nothing," she said quickly.

The truth bled from her eyes. It was half-amusing, half-infuriating that they had managed to snag an honest woman. He could see in her fear that she wouldn't hesitate to put herself back in the line of fire to see the gang brought down. He could hear it in the way she said 'gang stuff'.

"Is that what you'd tell the police? That you saw nothing?"

She flinched. "Yes. I'm just a working girl trying to make a better life for myself."

"I don't think so. I think you're the type of girl who has a self-sacrificing streak. I think that you'd run straight to the cops the moment you went out this door."

The woman snorted, turning her face away. "As if Sheriff Cunningham would do a damn thing about it. He thinks that you guys are some sort of break against even worse things."

Zane couldn't help but laugh at that. As he shook his head at the irony of that statement, something clicked in his mind. The smeared makeup, the glitter, the scent of sweat. The sweetness of perfume on her. She had said she was a working girl. He had the sudden image of her lying on her back, her curves laid bare before him, his hips between her thighs.

Then he thought of another man there and his wolf snarled in fury.

“A working girl, huh?” He shrugged. “I don’t mind partaking from time to time, so long as it’s from a reputable place that protects its girls.”

The woman stared at him for a long moment before her face flared red. She leapt to her feet, those green eyes glowing again. “I am not a hooker!”

She wasn’t?

“I happen to be a *waitress*,” she snarled at him, sounding like she was about to try to take off his face. “Not that it's any of *your* business—even if I was a hooker I wouldn't sleep with some sleazy *gangster.*"

Zane's hair bristled at that. He stepped closer to her, a growl in his throat. "Do waitresses usually wear glitter on their breasts?" He glanced at her exposed cleavage. She yanked the blanket back up, but not before it slipped down enough to show one juicy-looking nipple. "If you're not a prostitute, then you're a stripper."

She flinched as though it were an insult and not a profession.

"Whatever." He waved a hand. "That is hardly important. I have to decide what I'm going to do with you. I can't let you run off and tell everybody what happened today. Those idiots ought to have made sure there were no witnesses before taking out their mark. Would it help your conscious to know that it was a dealer of the tainted drugs that made their way into Coalfell recently?"

She didn't need to know that it was a vampire.

"If it was," she said, drawing herself up higher, "then they should have handed him over to the law and not killed him themselves! We have a law system for a reason—" She cut off and her eyes widened. Perhaps realizing she'd just admitted that she had, in fact, witnessed the murder that she had claimed not to see. She backed away from him, trembling again. "Your excuses don't make it any less murder, and there is no justification for that."

"Not even if one death means that two others survive? Or that children are spared abuse? What if it was a man who would kill his wife, and was killed specifically so he could not touch her?"

The woman opened her mouth and closed it again.

"What is your name?" he growled shortly. He didn't care what she thought—sometimes killing was the only way. Especially when it came to vampires.

She fidgeted on the spot. "Melanie."

Zane nodded at her. "People call me Thunder. You can call me Zane if you want."

The offer of his real name took him by surprise, but he pushed that away. He was just trying to make her feel more comfortable. He didn't like that she was staring at him with that fear still, as though expecting him to throw her on the desk or snap her neck. Not that he wouldn't mind having her on the desk, but not in her current state.

He frowned as he glanced at the door. A chorus of song was coming from the other side. He couldn't keep her locked up in this office. Not only would people talk, but the warehouse was a place where his men regularly got high and drunk. He ran a tight ship and he had men who he trusted to guard and protect her, but it was better to minimize the risks. He didn't want her to end up hurt—and he didn't want to have to kill off any idiot who hurt, or tried to hurt, her.

"Come on." He jerked toward the door. "I'm not going to keep you here. I've got a place where you'll... stay until I can figure out my next move. You will not be hurt or molested, I swear," he added. "But if you try to run, I will hunt you down."

Melanie stared at him for a moment longer before she nodded. He opened the door—and caught her by the tail as she tried to dart out. He seized the blanket again, wrapped her up, and carried her out of the warehouse. She snarled, tearing at the blanket as her claws found his skin and shredded it.

A smile tugged at his lips despite himself. What a feral kitty.

***

It was a good thing that he hadn't put windows in the basement like he had wanted. Zane carried Melanie, shoved into a cat-carrying case now, into his house. The basement wasn't exactly the most secure place, but it had a sturdy door and, with the lock he'd picked up, Melanie would be sequestered away for the time being.

"Here we are." Zane set the carrying case down at the base of the stairs and pulled out his tools. "I'll just get this lock in here and then you can settle into your new home."

He glanced into the carrying case. It had been difficult shoving Melanie in it, but once she was inside she hadn't made a noise. She pressed herself flat against the back wall, glaring at him while he worked. He moved quickly. There was no telling if the case would hold if Melanie tried to shift into human form. Besides that, he wanted to get her put away before...

"Zane?" His mother's voice came down the stairs. "Is that you?"

"Yeah, Ma," he called back, working faster. "Just give me a minute and—"

Of course, it was at that moment that Melanie decided to try to shift. The carrying case burst apart as she turned human. The edges cut into her arms and back, releasing a spray of blood into Zane's face. She bolted for the stairs and Zane pounced on her. He pinned her down, reaching to grab both her wrists.

"Help me!" she screamed, and Zane cursed.

“Stop that!” He slapped a hand over her mouth. “You’re just causing trouble!”

He dragged her to her feet. Melanie attempted to bite his hand and he moved it. She elbowed him, and he brought her closer to his body so she wouldn’t have to room to continue her attack. With one hand he yanked open the basement door just as there was a gasp above him.

“Zane Antony Burton, what in the name of all that’s holy are you doing?”

Zane flinched but ignored his mother as he shoved Melanie into the basement and slammed the door on her. He’d changed the handle into one that could lock and quickly locked her in. The deadbolt would have to wait. He stayed where he was for a moment, making sure that Melanie wouldn't be able to get out.

"You'd better have a good reason for this or I'm calling the cops right now," his mother hissed.

Zane let out a grunt, then turned on his heel. He took the stairs two at a time until he stood next to his mother. Her back hunched and her skin looked transparent it was so thin, but that didn't make her scowl any less intimidating.

"Ma, it's not like I'm keeping her as a slave," he protested weakly.

"You had better not be! I raised you better than this." She slapped his shoulder. "Now you go let that poor girl out of there or so help me—"

“She saw a couple of the men killing a vampire. But she doesn't know about vampires, so she thinks—”

His mother rolled her eyes. “Then tell her about vampires.”

“It’s not as simple as that and you know it,” Zane snapped at her. “Look, Ma, I brought her here for her safety. I can’t have her going around screaming about murder and I can’t keep her at any of the Brotherhood’s safe houses. Not when my men will start asking questions or, worse, Typhoon might find out about her. It’s just temporary.”

His mother glared at him, unconvinced.

Zane ran a hand through his hair. There wasn’t anything that he could say to convince her, not at the moment. The best he could hope for was that she at least trusted him enough not to call the cops. He ground his teeth for a moment, then yanked his phone from his pocket.

"What are you doing?" his mother snapped now.

"Calling Mary. She's about the same size and she," he gestured at the basement, indicating Melanie, "needs clothes." He paused a moment, noting the tremors in his mother's hands. "You need to go sit down, Ma. Did you take your medicines this morning?"

She snorted at him, still glaring. "Just make your call, Zane. Get that poor girl some clothes."

# Chapter Three

*Melanie*

It wasn't the dungeon she had been expecting. The room, though there were no windows for natural light to come through, was well-lit by an old-fashioned chandelier hanging from the ceiling. It was worn, the paint chipped, but the bits of glue on it showed recent work having been done in it. Everything in the basement was similar. Old, but usable and showing signs of repair.

The room was clean and dry, too. A little chill, but not terrible. There was a couch along one wall, facing a TV, and Melanie found another few blankets in a small end table beside it. She wrapped herself up in them, huddled on the couch.

The first question was where was she. As soon as she realized that there was no way out of the basement, Melanie's mind turned to the woman she had seen before. The one Zane called 'Ma'. She had been white-haired and feeble, bearing little resemblance to the robust wolf. But if she was his mother… did that mean that he was keeping her prisoner in his mother's house?

Was that little old lady with her white hair and wrinkled face part of the Savage Brotherhood?

There was movement outside of the door and Melanie leapt to her feet, eyes wide and face going pale. If it was the wolf again—her cat did *not* roll onto its back and purr at the thought—what would she do?

"Hello?" a thin voice called through the door. "Are you alright, dear?"

The wolf's mother. Melanie rushed to the door. "Please, let me out."

There was a beat. "My name is Felicia. What's yours?"

"Melanie. I'm just a waitress from Coalfell. I want to go home."

She waited, holding her breath as she listened, but there was no sound of the lock clicking open. Melanie pressed her hands to the door. If Felicia was part of the gang, then Melanie had no reason to trust her, or think that the lady would help her escape.

"Dear," Felicia said, sounding exhausted. "Tell me, have you been hurt at all?"

Melanie's shoulders slumped. Not physically, no. Well, nothing that would even bruise. She had a feeling that wasn't what Felicia was asking, though. "No," she said reluctantly.

"And why are you naked?"

Melanie looked down at herself. She had always been told, from the time she was a young girl, to keep her abilities to shift a secret. Growing up in Coalfell, the only shifters were really the Savage Brotherhood, and a handful of others that ended up working in places like the Chubby Kitty. Even the other felines she had met didn't always understand her, they being large predators and her being a small cat who was as much prey as predator.

"Dear, I know you're a shifter. I can smell it on you. You've got a bit of a peculiar scent, though… I'm an eagle myself… at least, I was once."

There was regret in Felicia's voice. Melanie hesitated a moment longer. "I lost my clothes trying to get away from them. Please, let me out. I don't want to die."

"Nobody is going to kill you, Melanie." Felicia's voice sounded weaker, more exhausted.

It reminded Melanie of when her father's health had taken a bad turn. Oh, God! How long had it been since she was meant to be home? Was he worried for her? What if he had fallen and couldn't get up? What if he had tried to cook something and set the house on fire?

"I need to get home."

Felicia hummed. "Zane knows what he is doing. He does important work. I can't risk that you will ruin that for him."

Important work? He led a gang for God's sake! How was that in any way important? What lies had Zane been feeding his mother, that he could lock up a naked woman and his mother would defend him?

"My boy is a good man," Felicia continued. "He's all I have left, and he looks after me."

Melanie closed her eyes and breathed in deeply. "I won't tell anybody what I saw. I just want to get home." Did she dare mention her father, or would the gang go after him if she did? "Please, let me—"

“Ma.” Zane’s deep, rumbling voice cut her off. “What are you doing? You shouldn’t be going down these stairs with your bad hip.”

He sounded so soft and concerned that all the curses Melanie wanted to throw at him for locking her up died on her tongue. She pressed her ear to the door as Felicia, her voice sounding a little stronger, told him that she was making sure Melanie was unharmed. He guided his mother away and Melanie returned to the couch. There would be no getting out that way...

When she heard footsteps on the stairs again, she shifted and raced to the door. There was some shuffling around, then the door swung open. Melanie jumped back to avoid it hitting her, then darted forward—only to ram face-first into a piece of wood that now blocked the entrance. Melanie backed up, blinking away stars as Zane laughed.

He tossed something into the room. It fell over Melanie, hiding her from view until she clawed her way out of it. She leapt at the wood, but Zane batted her back into the room and quickly shut the door.

"That was a valiant attempt," he called through the door as he locked it again. "But I'm not going to let you go that easily. Now, why don't you get dressed while I put this deadbolt in?"

Melanie snarled under her breath, but on closer inspection of what he had thrown at her, it was indeed clothing. She hesitated only a moment before she shifted back to human form and dressed. Having clothing on her body, even if the shirt had a V-neck that went halfway to her navel and the pants were tight enough to shift the position of her hips, was reassuring. She went back to the couch. Questions formed in her mind, but she didn't ask any of them as a saw blade appeared in the door.

***

It took Zane less than half an hour to install the deadbolt, making it even more difficult for her to break down the door. But Melanie didn't give up. While he had worked, she'd managed to steal a screwdriver from his toolbox. Now she stood on the end table, chipping away at the concrete wall near the top of the room.

Her arm ached with the effort and her forehead beaded with sweat. Fine powder coated her exposed chest and landed gritty in her teeth. She continued to chip away with all her strength, though. She didn’t need to open it up large enough to escape, just call for help.

The door opened, and she jumped and turned. There was no time to attempt to race out again, although from her last few failed attempts, she didn’t think that it would do any good anyway. She jumped off the end table as Zane came in, carrying a bowl of soup. The smell made Melanie's stomach rumble, but she didn’t reach for it.

He set the soup down next to the TV and moved to inspect her work. Melanie's fist clenched around the screwdriver. He was going to tie her up now. Patch up the concrete. Maybe put her feet in some and dump her in a lake. She swallowed dryly, backing away as she eyed him.

“So that’s what my mother was hearing. Huh.” Zane jumped onto the end table and took a closer look. “You know, there’s a foot of concrete you are going to have to dig through here... but by all means, keep going. I want to put a window there, anyway.”

He jumped back down and gave her a smirk. Her stomach did an odd sort of flipping thing, and her cat purred. It was as though the damn thing was trying to tell her that this was proof that Zane wasn’t dangerous.

“You might want to use a Philip’s rather than a Robertson; they’re pointier.” He winked at her then.

Melanie didn’t hesitate. With a rush of inexplicable emotion, she charged at him. Her hand lashed out, trying to skewer the wolf. He jumped lithely out of the way. She turned on her heel, jutting the screwdriver toward his neck. He grabbed her wrist and spun her all the way around. The screwdriver fell from her hand as he shoved her forward and yawned.

"Well, that was a pretty poor attempt." He picked up the screwdriver. "You are a rather stubborn kitty, aren't you? I don't want to have to tie you up, Melanie, but I will if necessary."

Melanie glared at him. "Go ahead and try! I'll scratch your face off. If you ever try touching me—"

"If I was going to hurt you, you'd be dead already," Zane interrupted. "And I understand your fears. Really, I do. I know what men like me are usually seen as. The kind that takes what they want regardless of anything else. But I will not hurt you, and I will not molest you. I was raised to respect women, not rape them."

Her cat rubbed against her chest. Melanie fought the sense of calm settling in her stomach. He wanted her to believe him, that didn't mean he was actually telling her the truth. She opened her mouth, closed it, and considered him. If she did believe him, it would settle a lot of her fears.

"What sort of gangster lives with his mother?" she asked, narrowing her eyes at him.

His gaze hardened. For a moment, Melanie was tempted to take it back. She liked seeing that she got some sort of a reaction from him, though. If he was genuine in saying that he wasn't going to hurt her, she at least needed to know what limits she had here. A chill stole down her spine, but her stupid cat still insisted that it was nothing to worry about.

“The kind of gangster who lives with his mother is the kind of gangster that is the alpha of one of the largest chapters of the Savage Brotherhood. He’s the kind of gangster whose father was murdered when he was a teen, and whose mother was permanently injured when her second husband beat her after finding out she could shift.”

Melanie's eyes widened at that. So that was what Felicia had meant when she said that she used to be an eagle.

Zane’s head lowered slightly, and he advanced on her, his eyes focused, his lips curling back again. Melanie backed against the wall and he pressed his hands to either side of her head, staring down at her.

"I killed him for that," he breathed. "And ended up in jail for ten years. Did you think that these tats were just for show?"

He gestured at the peek of tattoos on his arms and shoulders. She had been too worried about herself before to pay attention, but she remembered them now. They hadn't been any picture that she make out, but had been swirling and spiky. Prison tats.

"You know, she tried going to the police. But my step-dad? He was a cop. Every time she tried to get away or when she tried to press charges? It was like Sisyphus trying to push the bolder up to Olympus. Every time we thought there was progress… He deserved everything he got and none of your self-righteous sneers about law and justice will change that."

Melanie opened her mouth and shut it again, having nothing to say to that. Her cat nudged her, wanting her to speak, apologize for her earlier statement, something. She didn't dare, though. Not when the tightening in her stomach was becoming less about fear. It was clear that he loved his mother very much. Earlier, he had been so gentle with her.

But he was the alpha of the Ivywood chapter of the Savage Brotherhood. He wasn't some sort of woobie lover boy, he was a hardened killer. There was no reasoning with this sort of man.

Unless... He loved his mother and cared for her. Maybe she could try some sort of reverse Stockholm Syndrome thing, get him to be sympathetic to her and let her go? It was worth a shot at least. She swallowed hard as he backed away from her, his eyes still hard.

"I have to go home. For my father. I'm the only one he has, the only one who can take care of him. I've been trying to leave Coalfell for years and years, but he won't budge and every time I get enough money for it, he relapses anyway. He's in terrible health. If I don't go home, he could die. My father is a wonderful person. My mother died when I was a little girl and I'm all he has, and he's all I have. Please. Let me go home to him."

"You must care for him a lot, then."

"I do." Tears filled Melanie's eyes as she thought of all the horrible things that could have happened to her father, even in the short time she had been gone. "It's why I do what I do. Work full time at a cafe where I'm treated like I'm less than dirt, and then take off my clothes for a bunch of men who call me a slut just for selling what they're so desperate to buy. I don't even want to stay in Coalfell. I want to get away. From the town, from the gang, from all of it. Please. My father needs me."

Zane narrowed his eyes at her for a long time before he shook his head. "That's your problem."

He headed for the door. Melanie let out a hiss and leapt forward. She grabbed his arm and yanked him to a stop. "It is my problem! You know what isn't my problem? When a couple of idiots decide that they should kill someone in front of me! Cunningham wouldn't do anything about it even if I did tell him. I need to get home to my father! If it was you, and your mother needed you—"

"I'm a gangster." Zane ripped his arm away from her. "Why should I care about your father? If it was my mother, I wouldn't have gotten myself caught in the first place."

"Zane, please."

"Don't think I'm some sort of saint, Melanie, just because I love my mother. Now eat your soup before it gets cold."

He stalked out of the basement without another word. And even though she was dressed now, and she still sweated from her efforts at chipping away the concrete, she had never felt colder. She ought to have known that she wasn't going to get anywhere with him... she slowly crumpled to the floor, buried her face in her hands and started to cry.

There was no escaping it. She was going to be held prisoner here forever. Zane was never going to release her. Not when she was a threat to his freedom. He said it himself... he was never going to let himself end up in the same situation again. If he was in jail, who would be there to look after his mother? He wasn't going to risk that.

And so, she was never going to be free. The best she could hope for was that Ava would stop by her place, looking for her, and watch out for her dad... Because the only other thing they could do was perhaps have him come and be a prisoner with her. But what sort of life was that?

# Chapter Four

*Thunder*

"Hey, Cap'n!"

Zane stretched his back as he turned to greet his three closest friends, Kai, Tom, and Carl. His second, his enforcer, and his financial adviser. A fourth man, a new recruit named Bill or Phil or Gil or something like that, tagged after them. Kai, a huge buffalo shifter, smacked Zane on the back and plunked himself onto the couch in the lounge area of the warehouse.

"So, what's this I hear about you having a cute little pussycat locked up in your basement?" Kai grinned at him.

Zane glared in return, mentally cursing. So, the rumors had already spread, had they? He hadn't had

Melanie as a prisoner for more than a handful of days. He still didn't know what to do about her. Kai watched him closely as Tom and Carl plopped down beside him. Bill headed for the fridge.

"You don't have to worry about my pussycat," Zane told the three of them sternly. "She's connected to some business with Coalfell."

Kai stretched and settled back down. He put one of his arms over Tom's shoulders while the other stretched out on his other side. "Hey, I'd like to do some business with Coalfell if I can get a cat to keep all to myself."

Carl snorted. "Please. If you tried to lock up a cat, you'd end up with your dick bit off."

A wince answered these words and Kai withdrew his arms to shield his precious bits. “Whatever, Carl. So, why haven’t you told us about your kitty, Zane?”

Zane shot a glance at Bill, who had retrieved a pack of beers. He handed them out. Zane took his with a nod and focused on his friends again. “Because I didn’t.”

“Can’t argue with that,” Tom laughed as he took a swig of his beer. “Never thought you’d be one of those ‘straights’, though. I mean, keeping a woman captive? That’s some messed up stuff, bro.”

“She’s not my sex slave,” Zane snapped at him. “I have zero interest in her that way.” He deserved an award for managing to say that with a semi-believable tone. It was the biggest lie he had ever told. “I’m not interested in girls now.”

Tom grinned wickedly at him. “Ah, you’re trying out the other side of the fence, are you?”

Zane glared at him for a moment, but a grin tugged at his reluctant lips. “Unfortunately, no. If you want to be an alpha’s mate, you’ll have to find someone else.”

“If you’re worried about the dynamics, I’m a total bottom.” Tom winked, making Zane laugh.

Carl turned to him. “Really? How do you know? Like, I mean, don’t you like to take turns with it?”

Zane settled back with his beer, smiling as he felt himself relaxing. Just hanging out with the boys always helped clear his mind. He closed his eyes, allowing himself to simply enjoy their presence. Kai joined in the discussion now, the three of them arguing about what all the definitions of being a 'top' or a 'bottom' meant.

"Dude, whatever." Carl yawned. "I still say there's no such thing as a top or bottom, you take turns or it's just the same time all the time... Yo, I've been meaning to ask. Any of your friends willing to do casual? I've been thinking lately I might be bi, but how do I know unless I have sex with another guy, you know?"

Tom snorted. "And so, you want one of my friends?"

"If they're willing to go casual with me for some curious exploration. I'm not looking for a boyfriend."

"You guys aren't serious, are you?"

Zane opened his eyes, his gaze flicking to Bill. The man sat on the table, an uncomfortable look on his face. He frowned, but Bill didn't seem to notice. He glanced at Tom and Carl, that familiar, disgusted look starting to come onto his face.

"Are we going to actually do some work or just sit around and be gay?"

That was the wrong thing to say. The temperature of the room dropped several degrees. Zane's wolf snarled, and he slowly got to his feet. It was so hard to find proper recruits, really. It shouldn't be too much to ask that the shifters who wanted to be part of the gang weren't homophobic pieces of shit. Bill still didn't notice him, though, his gaze locked on Tom.

Tom's expression had completely smoothed out. He knew far better than Zane did, the type of action that could follow comments like that. His hands clenched but he remained calm—at least on the outside. "For your information, Brian, I'm gay all the time."

Bill—or Brian, apparently—made a choked noise of disgust in his throat. "Well... whatever. I don't have a problem with your lifestyle choices, but don't hit on me, or face the consequences."

That did it. Zane's wolf howled, and his fist flew. It made a satisfying crunch as it smacked into Brian's face. The recruit flew backward, his heels rolling up over his head. Kai, Carl and Tom all got to their feet. Tom grabbed his arm and pulled him back as Zane started to lunge again. The taste of blood was in his mouth and he wanted more.

Brian cowered on the floor, his hands clutching his broken nose.

"Homophobia isn't allowed in my chapter," Zane snarled, allowing Tom to keep him back. As the only gay man in the upper circle, Zane took his cues from Tom more often than not in these situations. He would not allow threats to his friends, though, not after what happened to his brother. "If you want to be an asshole, you can go crawling back to whatever mud pit you were born in."

Kai seized Brian's arm and pulled him back to his feet.

"I didn't mean anything by it," Brian whimpered, still cowering.

"You meant enough," Zane told him. "And you'd be damn lucky for a man as brave, strong and smart as Tom to be interested in your sniveling little corpse."

"Zane, that's enough." Tom pulled on his arm. "Let's just calm down and drink our beers, okay?"

Zane growled a final warning at Brian before allowing Tom to guide him away. Brian slunk into a corner, shoulders hunched as he downed his beer. What was he even sticking around for? Zane glowered at him as he sank back in his chair. He drummed his fingers against the arms of the chair, still feeling the thrum of energy beneath his skin. His wolf wanted blood.

"Change of plans," he said abruptly. "Those Southers are trying to muscle their way into Brotherhood territory. The five of us are going to go take care of them."

Brian's head jerked up, eyes going wide. Zane kept his gaze steady on him. It would be a good way to see if he was willing to trust the men and that he had their backs. If not, then there was no point keeping him. Zane grinned, allowing his teeth to start to shift as he continued staring at Brian.

"Let's get going."

***

The Southers lounged about their little clubhouse, laughing and talking to each other. Zane signaled for Kai and Tom to strike. They dropped in from either side, eliciting cries of shock. The Southers jumped to their feet and started reaching for their guns and knives. Kai punched their leader in the face. Carl gave a bellow as he charged in from the back. Half the Southers fled, and Kai and Tom quickly cut between the two groups.

Zane swung in, fists flying. His wolf snarled with pleasure as his fist struck into the face of a man who pulled a gun on him. Brian backed him up, blocking one of the Southers that came at him from an angle Zane intentionally left open. He drove into the midst of them, knocking hands aside as he clapped the Southers in the face and throat.

A man stabbed at Zane's throat. He easily sidestepped and hooked his arm around his attacker. He slammed his other palm against the man's elbow, forcing it the wrong way. A crack rang through the air. The man's legs buckled. Zane grabbed his other arm and twisted it sharply, popping the shoulder from its socket. The man dropped, screaming in pain.

Tom and Kai fought back to back, Carl swinging through the Southers to keep them separated and off-kilter. Zane laughed as he kneed someone in the groin and threw him into another of the Southers. Behind him, Brian gave a shout and darted through the mass to rabbit punch a man in the back of the neck. A gun clattered to the floor and went off as the man dropped. Tom turned, snorted, and punched two more men in the face.

The Southers panted, fighting to get free more than to subdue their enemies now, and with a single hand signal from Zane, the Brotherhood retreated, allowing them space. Zane smiled at them as he gazed at the fallen members of the rival gang. No deaths this time; it would serve as a warning without inciting the need for avenging fallen friends.

“This is territory for the Savage Brotherhood,” he said calmly as the Southers regrouped, panting and nursing their wounds. “You’d better clear out before things get bloodier. If you have any sense, you’ll pack up and leave Ivywood tonight.”

One of the men spat out a mouthful of blood. “Oh yeah? And who’s going to make us?”

Kai burst into laughter. “That’d be much more impressive if we hadn’t handed your ass to you just now. There’s five of us against what? Twenty of you? And you’ve got six still standing... we can take the rest of you down if that’s what you want. I haven't even broken a sweat."

The remaining Southers glanced at each other. A few of them looked like they would be more than willing to fight, but most them withdrew, looking at their feet, shuffling from side to side and wincing as their wounds pulled. Zane smiled, his wolf's need for violence sated.

"Let's go," he said to his men, turning on his heel. He sauntered back outside, whistling merrily.

They quickly returned to their motorcycles and tore off. All the way back to the warehouse, the men laughed and hooted congratulations to one another. Zane allowed himself the high of success, even though he knew it was temporary. This was just the start of it.

They'd have to hit Souther deals hard and fast. Make Ivywood too expensive a playground for them. Otherwise, they'd just regroup and cause more trouble.

Even if the vampires had been oddly quiet these last few months, that didn't mean he wanted to break their vigilance by having to deal with ordinary humans thinking they were bad asses.

He felt his phone vibrating in his pocket, and the Bluetooth speaker he'd installed in his helmet gave a series of beeps. Zane's heart stuttered—that was his mother's emergency signal. He pulled a fast U-turn on the street, earning him several angry horn blasts, but he ignored them. Kai turned slightly, meaning to follow, but Zane waved him on.

This was either about Melanie or something else. If it was Melanie, he didn't want anybody, even his friends, getting involved. And if it wasn't her? Images of his mother lying crumpled at the base of the stairs or passed out from the agony of a broken hip flew through his mind. If it was something else, they wouldn't be able to help anyway.

***

The thing that hit him the moment he stepped into the house was the overpowering stench of vampire. The sickening sweet smell of rotten fruit was so strong it made him gag. Instantly, adrenaline flooded his system. His stomach churned as he inhaled deeply. No scent of blood, but with a vampire that didn't mean anything.

His heart pounded as he entered the house slowly, watching every shadow for the vampire. There was no noise from down the stairs. Zane turned to the main room where there was the soft murmur of the TV. He crept in, ready to attack at a moment's notice.

He entered the living room to find a tall, thin man with impossibly pale features sitting in the single beam of sunlight streaming in from the windows. Zane froze at the familiar blue eyes and dark hair, that cruel smile twisting the thin face.

"Eldric."

"Hello, Zane." Eldric glanced to Zane's mother, who sat in a reclining armchair next to him. "He came quite quickly, didn't he? I must say, I'm quite impressed."

Typhoon was meant to have found out how vampires managed to walk around in broad daylight. Zane bit back a snarl as nausea started to creep up his throat. The whole daylight thing was one of the huge reasons why vampires didn't rule the world. If they weren't limited to the darkness of night, it became nearly impossible to tell them from a human. The scent was a giveaway, but scents could be faked easily enough.

There had been a new treaty written up between the two factions, but Eldric was never part of a vampire kingdom. He ran by his own rules—and those rules were that he did whatever he wanted.

"Ma, are you okay?" Zane inched closer to her. She was pale and shaking, but appeared unhurt.

Eldric chuckled as he picked up a teacup—part of Zane's mother's collection, that had belonged to her great-grandmother—and sipped at whatever brew was inside of it. Zane approached, still moving slowly. His wolf clawed at his chest, howling to be released, but to fight in his home? Against Eldric? The vampire played long games. He wouldn't be here unless he was absolutely certain he'd be able to get out again.

"What do you want, bloodsucker?"

Eldric clicked his tongue. "Is that any way to speak to an old friend?"

Zane snarled.

"Hmph. Well, if you're going to be like that." Eldric set his tea down. "I just wanted to let you know what my plans were, Zane my boy."

His mother flinched, and Zane started to move to put himself between her and Eldric. Before he could, though, Eldric had moved. Almost faster than Zane could see, he leapt across the table and seized his mother around the throat. Zane froze as his mother gave a short cry.

"I'm taking your mother, boy," Eldric continued, smiling horribly at him. "And I want thirty-thousand dollars by the end of the month... If I don't get what I want, Ma is going to end up on display next to dear dead Daddy."

Zane snarled and started forward, but another cry from his mother stopped him. He ground his teeth together, tense with fury and worry. There was no way to break Eldric's grip without hurting his mother. Hatred welled in him, so hard that his wolf howled with it. He forced himself to go back a step and Eldric's grip on his mother loosened.

"Why a month?" Zane growled. "That's an awfully long time."

Was this just a game? A way to torture him? Eldric had always had a peculiar fascination with Zane. He'd stopped the vampires who killed his father from killing him and had haunted him ever since. Never asking for repayment of the debt; always showing up when least expected and making Zane's life a living hell.

Eldric grinned at him. "Not when you take in recovery time, my boy. I want another little taste."

Zane bit back another snarl. So that was it? He just wanted to drink Zane's blood? No. It was more than that.

Perhaps he was genuine, wanting the money.

"Well? Roll up your sleeve unless you want Ma to sate my thirst."

"No!" Zane bit back the panic that threatened to consume him. He moved forward slowly, fighting the instinct to attack, and rolled up his sleeve. His lips curled back, but he kept his eyes on his mother, trying to reassure her without words as Eldric sank his teeth into his wrist.

Fiery pain shot through him. Zane bit back a cry of pain as Eldric started slurping greedily. His legs weakened, and he locked his knees, determined not to fall. His head started to spin. A sudden blow caught him on the chin and he fell back, hitting the floor hard.

“Shame I never got a taste of your brother.” Eldric licked his lips. “It must have been terrible for him… dying for loving another man. End of the month, Zane, or you lose the rest of your family.”

Eldric propelled his mother forward. Zane reached for his ankle, seeing an opportunity; Eldric kicked him in the face and everything spun around him. When his vision settled again, they were gone.

## Chapter Five

*Melanie*

What was going on? Melanie pressed her ear to the door. She thought she had heard voices, but now everything outside her prison was utterly quiet. She huffed, folding her arms as she stomped back to the TV. The damn thing was broken, and she couldn't figure out how to fix it. If Zane was going to keep her prisoner, the least he could do was give her some decent entertainment.

The door lock clicked, but Melanie didn't bother to attempt an escape. She looked over, ready to zing him with the perfect insult that she'd been working on—only to jump to her feet with a cry. Zane collapsed into the room. His tanned skin was almost white, bloody foam frothed at his mouth and his eyes were wide, taking on a yellow hue.

She had seen this before. In her friend who have overdosed and nearly died from it. Melanie pressed her hands to her mouth, shocked and frozen for a long moment. Zane pushed himself to his hands and knees and started to crawl toward her.

"Stay back," she warned, looking around for something to defend herself with. "I should have known that you'd be into drugs!"

Zane wiped his mouth, flinging the bits of foam away. "Not drugs. I need your help."

Though he panted, and his voice was weak, he still spoke clearly. Melanie stared at him, noting the trembles in his arms. Her stomach squeezed as she fought her natural inclination to help others. He was clearly on drugs, and he was a gangster. He was dangerous!

But when he groaned, his head falling forward, she couldn't help herself. She rushed forward to him, catching him before he slumped to the floor. His head knocked against her shoulder and his weight knocked her back, flat on the floor. He collapsed over her. With a soft moan, he turned his head and licked at her neck, making her squirm—she firmly told herself she did *not* like it, even as her cat bounced in her chest.

Zane laughed and put a hand on her chest, between her breasts. "I can feel her purring."

He snatched his hand back suddenly as if he had been burned and rolled off her. "Sorry."

"I—" Melanie cut herself off, not knowing how to respond to that.

"You need to suck it out. He drank, but then he bit me again."

"What are you—" Melanie's eyes widened as he offered his arm to her. There, one on the wrist and one near the elbow, were two half-moon bite marks. Two holes sunk in at the canines, but the bruising from the other teeth was clear. The one at the wrist was clean enough, but the elbow had green pus oozing from it, hardened into a crust around the edges.

"Suck it out," Zane ordered again. "Or I'll kill you."

He didn't seem to be in any state for killing, but there was something in his voice that made Melanie fully believe that he could do as he threatened. She adjusted herself, so that she had better access to the festering wound. His blood tasted like something dead. It made her gag as she started to suck out whatever that green stuff was. She spat out the mouthful as quickly as she could.

She repeated the process several times before the blood started to taste normal. Zane was limp at this time, and Melanie scrubbed off her tongue, feeling like she might throw up. What had he done to himself?

"Zane?" she shook him as his head lolled. Was he dead? Her heart started to pound.

His eyes snapped open. When they fixed on her, his pupils widened. His arms shot out, wrapping around her waist. Before she could even yelp, he'd pulled her down over him, staining her clothes with his blood, and kissed her—hard, deep and passionate. Melanie made a noise, mingled surprise and protest, and he released her.

"God," he breathed, one hand still tight on her wrist as he stared earnestly into her face. "You are gorgeous. Beautiful. Sublime. It's been so long since I've wanted a woman like I want you."

This time he tugged her down gently, slowly. His kiss wasn't as demanding but no less passionate as he cupped her face in his hands and nibbled at her lower lip. To her surprise, Melanie felt herself responding. Heat swirled in her core, her cat purred, and she leaned onto Zane's muscular chest, her hands playing over his taut skin.

*What am I doing? I haven't saved myself for years to throw it away on a gangster! Not to mention he's high and unable to give real consent right now.*

Melanie jerked away from him, panting as she broke the kiss.

Zane stared at her, moving up to caress her back then falling back with a groan. His eyes closed once more, and he shook his head hard. "No."

Her lips tingled with the after effects of the kiss. Her cat mewled angrily, clawing at her chest to get more. All her muscles trembled, heat pooling in her core.

“I’m sorry.” Zane’s words were soft and genuine. “I need you to call Hurricane.”

Another member of the gang? Melanie pressed her hands over his bleeding wounds. Shifters healed fast, but it was still shooting out gushes. It must be an artery. And he’d had her suck out… whatever had been in there. Her head started to spin.

She was jerked out of her thoughts when Zane snarled. His eyes were growing black and the foam at his mouth increased. A clawed hand lashed out, freezing inches from her face. Melanie flinched, throwing herself backward. Zane flipped over to his hands and feet. Fur started to layer his body and a low, deep growl emitted from his throat.

“Get out,” he snarled.

Melanie could hardly understand him behind his enlarging teeth. She backed away, her heart in her throat. All her instincts told her that running would only incite an attack.

"Call—" Zane convulsed, then looked up again. His eyes were utterly black, with a red rim around the edges. In a flash, he had changed into his wolf—huge, pitch-black. His fur stood on end, his whole body puffed up. With those red eyes, he looked like a hellhound.

He lunged.

Melanie stumbled back and slammed the door. It shook when he rammed into it. It held, though; there was a slight creaking, but that was it. She quickly locked it and raced upstairs, her heart in her throat. Who the hell was Hurricane?

When she emerged onto the first floor, she found it utterly empty except for a puddle of blood soaking into the carpet.

Melanie slapped her hands over her mouth, despite the blood still on them, to muffle her scream. Had he killed his mother? She recalled the wild, almost rabid look in his eyes. In that state of mind, hopped up on whatever he had taken, she wouldn't put it past him.

But no. The trail of blood led to the basement. This was his blood—there was no sign of Felicia, though. Had she gone out? Melanie noted a tea set on the coffee table, but even as she went to check if it was warm, a howl came from downstairs. It was the most inhuman and terrifying sound she had ever heard.

Hurricane.

She looked around wildly and found his phone on the floor next to the puddle of blood. More blood was smeared over it; it was open to a contact. Why hadn't he called this Hurricane himself?

Another howl. Had he simply run out of time?

Melanie shook her head, pushing that thought away, along with the crash of questions and rush of fear. It didn't matter if she didn't know exactly what was going on; Zane needed her, and she would help him in any way that she could. She wiped the blood off the phone's screen and tapped the call button.

***

The basement door was beginning to creak with Zane's repeated impacts by the time the front door flew open. A man charged in, eyes flashing as they landed on her. He wasn't as tall as Zane, but his muscular frame was a good few inches broader. Hurricane—there was no one else it could be—jerked his chin up. Melanie scrambled out of his way and crouched at the top of the stairs.

Hurricane unlocked the door. Melanie bit back a protest as the door swung open. Zane's black wolf lunged out, but Hurricane was quicker. Melanie didn't even see what he did, but in seconds he had pinned Zane to the floor, an arm around his throat while his big body bore down on him. He spoke rapidly and quietly, his tone soothing. Zane thrashed for a few more minutes before he went limp. His eyes closed, he let out a pained whimper, and he slowly melted back into his human form.

"There you go," Hurricane murmured. "You're okay. What do you need, Thunder? I brought Roxy if you need sex."

Roxy? Sex? Melanie let out a hiss, bringing the attention of the men below up to her. Hurricane narrowed his eyes, but Zane actually smiled. The red in his eyes was lessening, but there was still a dark look in them—lust, she realized. Melanie's nostrils flared as she looked away. Her cat snarled, sharpening its claws in preparation to rip out Roxy's eyes.

Which was ridiculous. Because there was certainly no reason for her to feel jealous of anybody.

"Roxy..." Zane murmured.

Melanie sprang to her feet and stomped into the living room. She stopped dead when she saw the woman there, sprinkling some sort of white powder into the blood puddle. It sucked up the blood eagerly, and Melanie had to turn her face away. She looked back, though, and studied the woman. This had to be Roxy. She was taller than Melanie, almost as tall as Hurricane. She wore a sleek red silk blouse and a pair of tight black slacks. Her hair was done up in a simple bun, but there was a sense of elegance around the woman that made Melanie feel a bit like a potato.

"So, you're Roxy?" Great. Her jealousy was bleeding through her words, plain as day. Melanie chewed on her lip.

Roxy gave her an unimpressed look. “What’s it to you?”

Melanie shrugged. “Just curious.”

Roxy returned to her work. “And who are you? If I knew Zane had a girl here already I wouldn’t have come. I don’t mind helping out when needed, but I don’t like doing it rabid.”

“Doing… rabid?”

“Well, yeah… Oh.” Roxy’s eyes widened as though just realizing something. A smirk wheedled its way over her face. “I see…”

“See what?” Melanie waited, but no explanation came forth.

“Roxy.” Hurricane called from behind them.

Melanie whirled to see Hurricane coming up the stairs, half-carrying Zane, who was wrapped in a blanket. His skin looked awfully pale, sweat beading his face. His eyes weren't red anymore, though, and the foam at his mouth was gone. She opened her mouth to ask how she could help, but closed it again quickly.

"You need me?" Roxy started to undo her blouse.

"What the hell are you doing? He needs to go to a hospital!" Melanie snarled at Roxy, making the other woman stare at her. "He's overdosed and—"

Zane spoke, his voice stronger than it had been. "I'm fine."

"Sure you are," Hurricane growled. He glared at Zane, but looked worried nonetheless. "He's being stubborn,

Roxy. Insists on riding it out without help."

Roxy nodded and buttoned her blouse again. Melanie glared at her still, a little angry those magnificent curves the other woman had appeared to be all natural. She'd make a killing at the Chubby Kitty and she wasn't even that chubby.

"He needs—" Melanie started again, turning toward the men. She cut off as she saw Zane's gaze rake over her. His desire was written all over his face, taking her breath away. So, he did want... but then, why wasn't he taking up Roxy's offer?

*He can't want me over her!*

"No hospital," he said low, but every word rang with authority.

Melanie shook her hormone-induced speechlessness off and put her hands on her hips. “You need something! If you won’t go to a hospital… what about morphine?”

Zane arched a brow but nodded.

Was she really doing this? Melanie held her breath for a moment before letting it out slowly. She nodded, determination overriding her good sense. She still had her father’s last prescription for morphine on her phone… It might take calling the doctor, but she could get it filled here, right? She would just have to tell the doctor that she’d lost the prescription or that the house had been broken into and their stock stolen.

She headed for the door, but Hurricane grabbed her arm, giving out a strangled protest. “You can’t just let prisoners—”

“I trust her,” Zane groaned.

Melanie’s jaw dropped. She wanted to demand what in all that was holy had convinced him of that, but there wasn’t time. She nodded at him and darted for the bathroom, where she scrubbed the blood off her hands before racing out of the house. She was halfway down the driveway when Roxy caught up and gestured to a sleek, sporty BMW. Melanie glared at her for a moment, but went to it.

To her immense displeasure, it was the most comfortable car she had ever sat in.

Roxy didn’t talk as she drove to the pharmacy. Melanie wished she would. Her disdain for this woman who was far prettier than her and apparently far richer wasn't strong enough to withstand the buffeting of the worries that seeped into her mind. She could take off right now. Go home to her father—was he okay? —but if she did that, would she ever find out what happened to Felicia?

Melanie pressed her palms into her eyes. She could almost smell Zane's blood still on her hands. And that more than anything stopped her from trying to fight off Roxy and escape.

Zane needed her. If she could help him, then she would... He loved his mother, and she had to help in every way she could to make sure he could get her back.

***

Hurricane lived in an honest-to-God mansion. The place was so immense, it probably could have housed all of Coalfell. Well, probably not that big, but it certainly felt like it to Melanie. Not that she spared much thought to the mansion since she first saw it.

Her hands and mind were busy watching after Zane. Hurricane had helped him into the house, put him in a metal-framed bed bolted to the floor, and promptly strapped him down with several leather bands. Melanie had almost protested, but remembered the senseless look in his eyes as he lunged at her in the house and didn't say a thing.

Now, she sat next to the bed, keeping an eye on the morphine drip. Hurricane had everything stocked up like a hospital, except for the drugs themselves. Melanie wasn't certain exactly what was going on anymore, but she was pretty damn sure that this wasn't an overdose after all. Had he been poisoned? Some sort of attack that made his wolf go crazy?

Roxy swept into the room. She wore an oversized sweater, which ought to have made her look dumpy. But no. She looked just as glamorous in it as she had looked in the silk blouse. She carried a tray with a fragrant tea and a handful of crackers, which she set down on the night table next to Melanie.

"You need to eat something," she said to Melanie's questioning look.

Melanie took one of the crackers and nibbled at it. "Have you found out anything about Felicia?"

"No. The blood in the house was definitely Thunder's. But it looks like

Felicia was kidnapped. We'll have to find out more when Thunder wakes up. He wasn't able to explain much more than who you were to Josef earlier." Roxy pulled one of the blankets a little higher on Zane's bare chest, looking worried. "One of these days his luck is going to run out."

Melanie didn't bother asking what that meant. "Do you think a rival gang took Felicia?"

"In a manner of speaking, I suppose." Roxy glanced up at her, snorted, and shook her head. "You're a shifter, but you don't know anything about the vampires, do you?"

"Vampires?" Melanie repeated blankly.

"Vampires. Vicious, undead monsters that go around sucking blood and killing people. The Savage Brotherhood is humanity's only line of defense against them. Those wounds on his arm? A vampire bit him. Twice. Once to drink his blood, the second time to poison him. Vampire venom is very dangerous to shifters. It makes us go crazy, and in many cases, it kills us. Zane's been bitten enough that he's built up somewhat of an immunity... But he's not invulnerable to it."

Melanie stared at her, uncertain whether she was joking or just on drugs. "Vampires."

"Vampires."

"Right. Of course, it's vampires."

Roxy rolled her eyes at Melanie's tone of disbelief. "You don't believe me now, but you will once Zane wakes up." The other woman circled the bed and leaned on the back of her chair, arching a manicured brow. “You know, not every prisoner would watch over their captor with such dedication. You got a bit of a BSDM kink there?”

Heat rushed to Melanie’s face. Her jaw dropped, and she protested incoherently. Roxy laughed and sashayed out of the room. Melanie glared at her, stuffing the handful of crackers into her mouth. There was nothing happening here—She was helping because that’s the kind of person she was.

It had nothing to do with her cat going crazy every time Zane was no longer in sight. Nothing at all.

# Chapter Six

*Thunder*

A familiar buzz of heat and energy ran under his skin as he woke up. Zane licked his lips, an oddly salty taste in his mouth. When he rolled his head to one side, he saw an empty IV drip hanging by the bed. The needle had been removed from his skin, a crusted scab the only indication it had been there.

Zane lay still, knowing from experience that trying to move, only to find himself strapped down, would make his wolf go crazy and relapse back into the rabid fear of the vampire venom. His heart thrummed, and he had to admit that he had been damn lucky to get out of this one alive. If Melanie hadn't been there to suck the venom from his system, he wouldn't have gone rabid—he'd have just died.

When a vampire bit a shifter, the average reaction was either going rabid or dying, depending on how much venom was in the system. For the survivors, when the rabidity passed, they'd have a brief time of feeling like they were back to full strength only to fall so ill that they couldn't remember their own name.

He was a little different. He went rabid quick, healed quick, and never had that second relapse. Instead, it left him with a case of raging hormones that demanded sometimes up to a week in bed with a handful of women. His stamina was always... very high after an attack like this.

Inhaling softly, he caught the sweet scent of a feline nearby. His head turned so fast that he got a crick in his neck.

Melanie sat in a chair nearby, her arms pillowing her head as she leaned on the arm. Her dark hair tousled around her, having not seen a brush in several days now. She made the most adorable little snores he had ever heard, and Zane couldn't help but smile. Those were just like the sounds she had made while he kissed her neck and entered her…

Wait.

No.

Zane let out an annoyed breath. He had been in no condition to make love. Even if he had been, Melanie didn't want anything to do with him. Right?

So, he must have imagined the whole thing.

Disappointment hit hard, but he tried to shove it aside. He could feel the blanket wrapped around him tenting at his nether regions, but he was too used to this to be embarrassed by it. His need would be distracting for a while, but it was nothing he couldn't handle if Melanie didn't want to help him get through it.

Wait, *what*? Where had that come from? Yeah, she was attractive, but she wasn't the only option available. Take Roxy, for example. She made her living out of sex, having chosen the lifestyle and working for a reputable organization. She chose her clients and when and how she delivered the 'product'. He trusted that she wasn't being manipulated into it. He had, from time to time, paid for her services. She was beautiful, sexy, and knew what she was doing.

And she was right there. Roxy, her hair done up in braids and wearing a stunning wrap dress that emphasized her bounteous curves, sauntered into the room carrying a tray. Her eyes widened when she saw he was awake and a smile crossed her face.

“You’re finally awake. Good. Josef’s been worried.” Roxy set the tray down on the nightstand and glanced at the still-sleeping Melanie and lowered her voice. “She’s been here the whole time. Fretting like a mother hen.”

Well, his reaction to her was not at all the way a son looked at his mother. Zane shifted uncomfortably and lifted one hand, still bound, to point at the leather straps holding him down. “Care to untie me?”

Roxy stared at him for a moment, then nodded. Zane kept himself relaxed as she undid the straps. The nervous energy still making his wolf pace dissipated once he was free, and he slowly sat up and swung his legs off the bed. He still felt a little weak from the vampire attack, but it was nothing that he couldn’t handle. That he woke up meant the worst had passed. He’d be able to handle the rest.

“My oh my,” Roxy said dryly, glancing at where the blanket, still covering him, tented. “Looks like you need some help taking care of those after effects...”

Zane cleared his throat, glancing away. Heat crept up his cheeks and he piled the blanket over his lap. Roxy rose her eyes at him, and when he glanced at Melanie, a smirk spread over her face. He opened his mouth to tell her that he didn't require her services, but before he could, she had undone the tie on her dress and let it fall open.

Out of instinct, Zane's head swiveled, and he looked up and down her body. His loins were already tight and looking at her, they actually throbbed.

"Roxanne..."

Of course, it was his voice that made Melanie wake with a start. She bolted upright, eyes wide and bleary. They sharpened up a hell of a lot when they landed on Roxy's exposed body, with her small, lacy bra and pantie set. Melanie's eyes bulged.

“What the fuck do you think you’re doing? He’s in no shape for sex!”

“Melanie,” Zane started.

“Actually, kitten,” Roxanne interrupted, “after being attacked by a vampire, it’s beneficial for a shifter to have sex and lots of it. Especially when he’s a man like Thunder here. It just makes it… easier, I suppose, to recover. Of course, if you want to join us you’re welcome to.” She winked. “It’s hard taking care of a viral man hopped up on vampire venom on my own.”

Melanie choked and spluttered, her face going beet red. “You are not having sex with him!”

Zane couldn’t repress a chuckle. Whether it was her being protective or possessive, he didn’t really care. His wolf relaxed further. Its tail wagged, and it bowed in Melanie's direction, an invitation to play. When she shot him a glare, he only grinned wider. "I think I'm a grown man who can decide for himself whether to have sex or not."

Melanie's face flared beet red, but she turned her glare at him. "You have been unconscious for a week. You need food, liquids, and if there is any exercise, it's gotta be gentle and not sex. I don't know what she's going on about vampires, but it's only common sense."

"Since when do you know about vampires?" Zane frowned at Melanie as he spoke.

Melanie folded her arms and glared at him.

"I told her," Roxanne told him. "I thought she deserved to know what she was getting mixed up in. I'm not sure she believes me yet, though."

"I don't," Melanie shot at her, but there was a strange way she was holding herself, a stiff way that made Zane think she was exaggerating her disbelief.

He stood, holding the blanket around his waist. His legs were a little shaky, but still strong enough to hold him up. The thing about being asleep for a week, processing the venom in his system, was that he always woke up with more energy than he knew what to do with. He walked around the room a little, hoping to soften his hardness, but it was no use. He sighed as he returned to the bed and sat down.

"Rox, go get Hurricane, will you?" Maybe if he talked about other things, it would distract his body from its desires.

Roxy nodded and swept from the room, while Melanie spluttered. She slammed her fist down on the bed, bringing Zane's attention back to her. "I am not going to get involved in some group sex orgy thing!"

"Okay. Neither am I."

Melanie's brow furrowed.

Zane laughed, but quickly sobered. "I'm the alpha of the Ivywood chapter of the Savage Brotherhood and a vampire attacked my home. He took my mother." A sharp, panicked pain shot through his heart, but he swallowed it down. Eldric wouldn't hurt his mother when he was after money, would he? "I can't go to the gang; it'd make me look weak. So I need Hurricane's help on this one."

"Vampires. Are they a rival gang?"

Zane rolled his eyes. "No. You know stories about vampires? Dracula, Carmilla, all that? They're those type of vampires. Well… not exactly, but close enough. When a human's bitten, they turn into a vampire. If a shifter is bitten, they go rabid. The animal inside loses all reason and lashes out at anything that moves. Lots of times this can be circumvented with sex, if the rabidity hasn't progressed too far."

Melanie shifted on the spot, looking uncomfortable. "Well… that's what Ava told me when I called her to get her to check on my dad for me. You could have let me phone her earlier," she added, glaring at him, "then at least I'd have known that she brought my dad to her place!"

"Tornado is the alpha of the Coalfell chapter. If he knew that I had a prisoner from Coalfell, especially his mate's best friend, there would be a lot of trouble." He frowned at her. "I hope you didn't say anything about being a prisoner."

"Of course I did!" Melanie rolled her eyes. "And then I told her that I was staying to look after you like a fucking idiot."

He wasn't certain why the swear coming out of her mouth was so amusing. He had to grin, though. "And so, Ava told you about vampires... and you still don't believe her."

"I don't know. I mean... vampires... But there has to be a reason why she's okay with being mated to a gang leader..."

Hurricane and Roxy came back into the room and Zane let out a sigh of relief. The thought crossed his mind that maybe he ought to get dressed first, but he shook it off. They were shifters. Nakedness was a part of the deal. There was no reason why he needed to get dressed.

"Glad to see you awake." Hurricane gave him a thin smile.

The two of them weren't close, not really, but Zane knew that he could always count on him. He had been part of the gang for a long time, until he was ousted by Typhoon's orders. Despite that, he still helped the gang when he could. His house wasn't charmed against vampires like the safe houses would be, but it was out of the way and made for a convenient place to crash when things were getting hairy. Not to mention he was a billionaire, and the money helped in the quest against vampires.

Zane trusted him more than any member of his gang, even his friends. Hurricane had been his brother's best friend; just before his brother died, he had told Zane that he'd confessed a long-burning love for Hurricane to him, and Hurricane had turned him down, but with a lot more grace and respect than his brother was used to. And then, he had nearly been beaten to death trying to save him.

There was something about that shared grief that had bonded the two of them. They were like brothers. Not close, but always there for each other.

Hurricane gripped his shoulder. "Glad to see you up."

"Yeah. Thanks for keeping me here. And I'm going to need more help. The vampire that attacked me? It was

Eldric. He took my mother and wants money to let her go."

Hurricane's eyes widened. Roxy and Melanie glanced at each other, their expressions confused, but neither spoke. Zane was grateful. He didn't want to get into all the messiness about his relationship and past with Eldric right now. There was already enough to worry about.

"Typhoon can't find out about it," he added. "A compromised alpha doesn't last long."

Hurricane nodded, his brow furrowed. "I can get the money easy, but this is clearly a trap. Eldric only shows up when he wants to cause trouble."

"Don't I know it," Zane muttered darkly. His fists clenched. "I just have to figure out what his endgame is here.

Why he came at me for that money and if he really wants it. The vampires are still in a state of disarray since they settled with that new king down near Coalfell. A lot of the other kingdoms are refusing to recognize the new treaty, saying they had nothing to do with the destruction of the old one. They're on their best behavior, though. The chaos is something that Eldric thrives on. For all I know, he's trying to stir things up so he can get his own kingdom."

It was unlikely, though. Eldric had never shown any interest in ruling anything himself. They needed to figure out his endgame, though.

Hurricane glanced at him warily. Zane couldn't tell what he was thinking, but he didn't protest. Which was a good thing, because the priority here was to get his mother back. After that, if he could kill Eldric, it would be a cherry on top. He couldn't risk his mother's safety for revenge, though. Even though Eldric had killed his father and bitten his step-father, forcing Zane to kill him. Yes, his step-father had been a horrible man, and if Zane had known that he was beating his mother, he would have killed the man in a heartbeat. The fact was, though, that if he hadn't been in the process of turning into a vampire, he never would have had the strength to hurt Zane's mother so badly that she lost her ability to shift into her eagle form.

"So, you're going to pay him and get Felicia back, right?" Melanie asked. There were dark circles under her eyes that he hadn't noticed before.

Zane nodded. He frowned, then sighed. "You should get out of this before you get mixed up further. Go home to Coalfell and your father. Forget about vampires and everything you saw… The Brotherhood is the only defense against vampires, and the man you saw those two idiots kill was a vampire. Just go about your life pretending you know nothing. It will be much safer for you."

"It's too late for that," Roxanne argued. All the heads swiveled to her. "Eldric was in your house, he probably knows all about her. Leaving now would only put her father in danger."

Melanie shivered. "Then what do you suggest I do?"

"Stay here for a while. At least get some sleep. You've hardly closed your eyes since we brought Zane back."

Melanie flushed, but she nodded slowly. She yawned as she got out of the chair, stretching her back out (which, Zane noticed, made her breasts pop out that much more. God, but she was beautiful). She yawned again, and Roxy gestured for her to follow her out. It left the two men alone, and Hurricane leveled him with a concerned look.

"How long do you have before you need to pay him?"

"The end of the month."

Hurricane nodded. "Then you have time. If you don't want Roxy, I'll call in another of the girls. You need to rest up and take care of things so you're at full strength when you go after Eldric—Ivywood needs its alpha, especially since Typhoon's so busy dealing with all the kings right now."

"Yeah, I know," Zane snapped at him. "I'm not going to do anything stupid. But I will do whatever is necessary to get my mother back, Hurricane. She comes first."

Hurricane nodded slowly. "Yeah. I know. Now, I'm going to call—"

"No." Zane scowled as he bunched up the blankets over his hips more. "I don't need a woman, Hurricane. I'll handle this myself."

Hurricane arched a brow skeptically, but didn't say anything. He clapped Zane on the shoulder and shrugged. "I'll let you have some privacy, then. You can have the fourth room on the left down the hall if you want a bigger bed—you'll also have access to my online collection if you want."

Zane snorted as Hurricane left the room, shutting the door behind him. The thought of porn wasn't appealing to

Zane. As he settled back on the bed, taking himself in his hand to release the pressure that was even more acute since Melanie left the room, all he could think of was her and her face. His eyes drifted shut and he brought up the dreams of them together, sighing as he wished he had the real thing snuggled beside him, warm and receptive, with her ruby lips and bright eyes.

# Chapter Seven

*Melanie*

Her cat hissed and spat and clawed at her chest, as though she still needed to be worried about Zane's health. He was awake, he was horny—he was fine. She needed to put him out of her mind and get some sleep.

Melanie rolled over, trying to get comfortable enough to let exhaustion take her away. Honestly, she needed to just stop thinking about him altogether. After all, she had no reason to keep thinking about Zane and his handsome face and those bounteous muscles that flexed and bulged when he moved. Or about that tent in the blankets.

There was a soft knock on the door. Melanie rolled out of bed, grumbling under her breath. What did

Roxy want with her now? She yanked open the door—and stopped dead. It wasn't Roxy standing on the other side of the door. It was Zane. He gave her a grin that had something tightening inside of her and she made a strangled noise of protest.

"Hey." His gaze swept over her, clad in the loose-fitting nightdress that did nothing for her. And yet his gaze heated, causing a pressure to build between her legs. She pressed her thighs together, trying to stop her panties from getting wet at a simple glance. Zane's smile returned to her face. "I just wanted to thank you for looking out for me."

He was shirtless but wore a pair of sweats. The bulge in them was more tamed than it had been in the bed, but Melanie still couldn't stop herself from glancing down, out of pure curiosity.

Heat flared through her, especially her face. "Well… you're welcome, I guess."

Zane leaned on the door frame. "I'm curious. Why would you do that for someone you don't even like? I was holding you prisoner and you still sat at my bedside, nursing me back to health."

"Well, I wasn't going to leave you alone while you were dying."

"I wasn't dying… and maybe I like being alone."

Melanie shivered. Why did his tone hint at something far bigger than the moment here and now?

Zane shrugged, stepping back slightly. Her cat mewled in distress, though she tried to keep it from her face. Seriously, now wasn't the time for her to start going crazy over a guy. He had said it himself. She didn't even like him... so then why was she so concerned for him, why did she want him to wrap her in his big, strong arms and never let her go?

"If I go home," she blurted as he started to turn, "will the vampires come after me and my dad?"

Zane hesitated a moment, then shrugged. "Maybe. They shouldn't, but vampires are unpredictable. Tornado can put men on a protective detail on you if you're worried."

She scowled at him. Protected by a bunch of gangsters. Right. Like that was going to happen. "You mean like those two who brought me to you in the first place?"

Zane chuckled at that. He stepped forward again, his mouth opening. But whatever he was going to say died in his throat. His gaze moved to her lips and he suddenly leaned to her. He caught her mouth in a kiss, immediately teasing open her lips to thrust his tongue into her. Normally that sort of behavior would be a turnoff, but Melanie felt herself responding deeply. Her fingers clenched into her nightdress, wanting to rip it over her head. Heat sparked under her skin and her core tightened.

What did 'someone special' even mean? She had been saving herself, and here was a man whose kisses alone were orgasmic. He promised a lot in bed, and she wanted to feel it all.

Just as she made a move to wrap her arms around him, he pulled back. Melanie's chest heaved as she licked her lips, heat simmering through her body now. Her cat mewled, demanding more.

She wasn't in any mood to fight it, either. Her lips tingled with the desire to be pressed into Zane's and her fingers twitched.

"Sorry." He gave her an apologetic grin. "I shouldn't have– "

She didn't want his apologies. She wanted *him*. With a snarl, she seized his arms and pulled him to her. The kiss was deeper than before, fire burning through her, her cat purring with desire. Zane wrapped his arms around her waist and lifted her up and out of the way as he entered the room and closed the door. He turned her, pressing her into the wall, while he ground his hard length against her.

A shiver ran down her spine as he moved to her neck. She held him tightly as she lifted one leg over his hip, opening herself to him. The friction between their clothes made her shiver more. Her neck tightened under his ministrations, and when one of his big hands cupped her breast, she let out a small cry of pained pleasure. It felt so good, she didn't want it to stop.

"I'm a virgin," she blurted as his free hand started to pull her nightdress out of the way.

He froze. Melanie held her breath, afraid suddenly that he was going to tell her that he didn't do virgins, that he only wanted experienced women who could give him pleasure.

Zane pulled back, his brow wrinkled. "You're a virgin?"

Melanie nodded.

"Oh... I'm sorry, I shouldn't be—"

He tried to pull away, but she held him fast. “You shouldn’t be what?”

A flush crept up Zane’s tanned cheeks. “Your first time should be special. With someone that you care about. Not a fling with someone you don’t even like.”

He was right, of course, but when Melanie's hands started to loosen, her cat let out a shriek and started to claw at her chest so hard that she winced. She shook her head, not letting go of him. It was her body, it was her choice.

“Maybe this is special, because I know that you won’t leave me hanging. There’s a lot of guys out there that would jump at the chance for a virgin simply because she’s a virgin. I know that I don’t know enough to make it good for you, but I... I want...”

He swallowed hard. “I would do my best, yes. Not because you’re a virgin, but I like to give pleasure to my partners. But you have to understand that being bitten by a vampire leaves me very desirous. This isn’t because I feel any special connection to you. There are other women, I don’t need you.”

She wasn’t certain if that was meant to reassure her or dissuade her. In any case, her cat snarled at the thought of him with anybody else and she clutched him tighter.

“You came to me, Zane. You refused Roxy and you came to me. That means you want me. I want you, too.” She pushed at his chest, her gaze locked on his. He allowed her to walk him back to the bed, and when his legs hit the edge and he fell back, she climbed over him, straddling him. Her nightdress bunched up at her hips. “I am going to claim you now.”

He thrust his hips up, grinding against her again. She shuddered, her head falling back as sparks filled her core. God! How did he know exactly how to touch her—without even really touching her?

“Claim me,” Zane panted, his hands on her hips as he looped his thumbs into her panties. “I don’t do forever, Melanie. This is a day, a week, whatever. But it ends, and it ends soon.”

Melanie knew that should have been her warning. She knew she should have gone running at that. Her first time with a man that didn’t want a relationship, just wanted the sex, was a man that she should kick to the curb. He said himself that he could have had any other woman in a heartbeat. But her cat yowled with demands, her chest ached and the heat in her body demanded sating.

"I don't do gangsters. Of course it ends soon," she bit back, then threw herself over him and kissed him.

Their tongues tangled. Their bodies pressed together, so tightly Melanie wasn't certain if the heat that filled her came from her or him. His mouth was hungry and demanding on hers, his hands wandering all over her. He grasped her ass as a growl rumbled in his chest. Melanie found herself with her hands on the bed, bracing herself up, and a sudden flash of panic shot through her. What was she supposed to do now?

Zane seemed to sense her panic, because he broke the kiss and rolled, so they were laying side-by-side. He stroked her cheek and smiled. “You can change your mind. You know that, right?”

Melanie fidgeted and nodded, more heat rushing to her face. “I know that.”

“And if you don’t like something, you tell me. And if you like something, you can tell me to keep going.” He winked at her. “The key to good sex is communication... and I don’t suppose you have condoms on you?”

She hadn’t even thought about protection. She shook her head and glanced away. What must he be thinking of her right now?

Zane pressed a light kiss to her lips before he got out of the bed. “I’ll go get some, then. And a few other things, maybe... I want this to be good for you, after all."

He left her alone and Melanie rolled onto her back. Her body still ached with need, thrumming with desire. She imagined him between her legs, deep inside of her, and she waited. In the past, whenever she had been with a guy and it got to this point, she would be filled with a sinking, sick feeling that left her with a bitter taste in her mouth. But here, now, all she had was desire.

A smile crossed her lips as she slipped her panties off and tossed them to the floor. She tucked her nightdress between her legs and rolled over, watching the door eagerly. Zane came through moments later, carrying a small bag. He headed back to the bed and turned it over. Out tumbled a roll of condoms, a bottle of lube, and several toys. Melanie reached for a package of beads the boasted a sterile environment and warned to only use them once.

"I'm not sure I want to use these," she said.

Zane shrugged. "Then we won't use them."

He smiled as he stripped off his pants. He sprang to attention right away and Melanie stifled a gasp. She had the insane urge to avert her gaze, as though seeing each other wasn't the point of this. Her cat purred.

Zane chuckled as he ripped open a condom and rolled it on. "I tried taking care of myself earlier, but I'm afraid it didn't do much good... I'll hold out, though, until you're ready for me."

Melanie flushed, nodded, and picked up a vibrator. Was he planning on using that on her first? Wouldn't it be painful for him to deny himself while he was pleasuring her like that? Her face fell into a frown as she flicked the vibrator on and looked up at him. His eyes were dark with lust, a tremor in his arms as he stared down at her.

Even though her cat yowled and mewled and demanded him, there was something in her that shied back from it. Melanie took a deep breath and moved to a sitting position. She wanted this. That was for damn certain. But maybe she just wanted to play...

Zane sat next to her, brow furrowed. "Are you okay?"

Melanie scowled and shrugged. "I want this. I do. But my mind... it won't shut up. I'm not sure how I want this to happen."

Zane considered her for a moment, then nodded. "Okay." He brushed her hair from her face and brushed his lips over her cheekbone. "Then let me have you the way I want."

That sounded like a good idea. Melanie let out a shuddering breath and nodded. Zane's hands roamed over her, lightly, gently, before he tugged her nightdress up. His fingers brushed over her stomach as he pulled it out of the way. When her breasts were exposed, he kissed first one and then the other. Her nipples pearled under his attention, and he pulled her nightdress completely off. He tossed it to the floor and continued to suck on her nipples. Something pulled and snapped inside of her and she leaned her head back, her eyes starting to drift shut.

“Spread your legs a little,” he ordered her, and she obeyed. His fingers slipped between her thighs. They brushed lightly over her clit, making a shiver shoot down her legs, then settled into a soft, circular motion.

Melanie's whole body seemed to tighten under his attention. She let out a soft moan as Zane continued his work, stroking her with one hand, pushing the fingers of his other inside of her while his mouth moved from her breasts to her neck to her mouth then back to her neck. Melanie clenched her hands at her sides, struggling to keep her body motionless while her hips moved of their own accord, rolling over his hands, trying to increase the pressure at times while decreasing it at others.

"God." Zane suddenly cursed, in a soft, pained whisper. "It hurts to be this close to you. To smell you, to taste you and not be inside of you."

Melanie started to move to lie back. "I'm ready for— "

"No, you're not."

"But— "

"You're wet, but you haven't relaxed at all. If I entered you now, I'd just hurt you." Zane nipped at her throat and with a groan, he gripped himself with one hand. "I can deal, I just have to..."

He trailed off and Melanie licked her lips. Her whole body felt like it was on edge, trembling with need. She wanted him inside of her. Right now. But she also didn't want to be hurt. With a frustrated growl, she reached so her hand joined his. She stroked him, twisting her hand like the women in the pornos she sometimes indulged in. She wanted him to feel good!

"Maybe you just need to... you know... use my mouth," she said, feeling a little awkward.

Zane made a face. "I don't like blowjobs. They get the job done, but it's just... I don't know. I just don't like them."

Melanie gaped at him. She didn't realize that was even an option. But then, it made sense. Different people liked different things. If he didn't like that, then he had to have other things that he did like... right? She frowned as she continued to stroke him and realized that he had let himself go. His head leaned back, and he thrust his hips in a gentle rhythm, moaning.

"I like that," he murmured. "A little faster."

With a grin, Melanie did as he said. She watched his face as she tugged on him, watching as his chest heaved and his throat worked. Seeing his pleasure made her want more of her own. She grabbed the vibrator again and flicked it on, rubbing it between her thighs.

Zane's eyes flew open. He snatched her wrists, stopping her. Melanie arched a brow at him and he deftly took the vibrator from her.

"That's my part," he growled at her. "Watching your eyes roll into the back of your head and hearing those little noises you make as your orgasm creeps up on you. That's *my job,* not yours."

Melanie licked her lips, at a loss for words. Zane growled again, the sound playful and predatory, and with a single motion, he pushed her back onto the bed. He started on her again, using the vibrator against her clit while he kissed up one thigh and down the other. Everything tightened to a point of pain inside of her and she clung to the bed, crying out.

"Do you like that?" he asked her, using his tongue on her clit now while the vibrator sunk deep inside her.

"Yes. Don't stop," she begged, kicking out one of her legs and then bringing it back. It was too much. Too powerful. And yet she wanted more. She gripped the vibrator as it hit the nerves inside of her, and she wanted it to be Zane there instead. She cried out again, her back arching and her core clenching. A feeling like a hot explosion went off in her core and she clawed at the blankets, mewling.

Zane laughed, kissed her hip, and began thrusting in and out of her with the vibrator.

Melanie hadn't known what multiple orgasms really were until she lay in that bed, helpless to Zane's skill and her own pleasure. Each explosion was more powerful than the last. The vibrator felt smaller and smaller, until it simply wasn't enough anymore. By that time, she was begging Zane. He kissed her, long and deep, before he entered.

If the movement with the toys was gentle, he was not. He thrust into her like a man possessed, rocking hard and fast. Melanie clung to him, biting her tongue to keep from screaming as he brought her to a new orgasm within seconds. He stared down at her, his eyes dark with lust, his teeth bared, and she knew why he said he needed to get her ready before he took her.

Her clit throbbed. Melanie came again twice before Zane stopped—unfinished—and used the lube on her, to make sure she stayed wet, and started up again. For what felt like hours, he thrust in again and again, stopping occasionally for her to catch her breath only to start again. It was too much. Melanie clung to him, her fingers clawing at his back as he went as deep as he could with every thrust.

Suddenly, his body went tense. His movement became jerky. She could feel him finish, and relief mingled with disappointment—she knew she wouldn't have been able to last much longer.

When he collapsed over her, growling and panting, she tangled her fingers in his hair and closed her eyes. Her whole body ached from the repeated orgasms and as she finally relaxed, a wave of drowsiness came over her.

"Thank you," Zane whispered, kissing her neck gently again.

"No problem," she murmured back, then opened her eyes and looked up at him. "Was it good for you?"

# Chapter Eight

*Thunder*

He hadn't meant to batter her body for so long. But as soon as he was inside of her, the feeling of how right it was took hold, and he couldn't let himself stop. Not when he knew that this was the only time he was going to have her. He wished he knew how she felt, although by the satisfied, glowing expression on her face, he had some idea.

He relaxed and chuckled lightly at her question. "It was good. And you?"

"Better than I expected," she admitted, stretching. "Is it always like that?"

"No. I was more..." He struggled to find the right word. "Exuberant than normal. Usually I'd have finished you off a couple times then taken you softer. And not as long. Vampire venom. It's like Viagra on steroids after I've left the rabid stage."

Melanie yawned. "Oh. Well... it was good. I liked it. But I'm so sleepy now..."

"Sex does that." Zane reluctantly left her and swung out of bed. "I have to go now. I'll be back."

Melanie frowned at him. A hurt look crossed her face, but she shrugged and rolled over. "I'll be sleeping."

There was a carefully unconcerned tone to her voice that made Zane flinch. He opened his mouth to explain, but what was there to explain? They had already established that this wasn't anything permanent. He had his business that he had to take care of and she knew that. By now, Hurricane would have Eldric's money. And Zane knew he needed to get this taken care of right away. He might not be back to full strength, but every minute that passed was a minute that Eldric could be tormenting his mother.

And he'd go alone. Hurricane would want to go with him, but to bring even one other person would put Eldric on edge. Yeah, it could be a trap to lure Zane to vampire territory, so he could kill him without repercussion as stated by the treaty, but since when had Eldric cared about the treaty?

Zane kissed Melanie's bare shoulder one last time. "I will be back," he promised, and slipped away.

***

As predicted, Hurricane wanted to join him on his mission, but Zane refused to let him come. He drove his motorcycle out of Ivywood with the money stashed in the saddlebags of his bike. His wolf snarled, wanting to go forward and rescue his mother while at the same time pulling back, wanting to go back to Melanie. It had been a while since his wolf pulled at him to be with a woman like this, and never this strong.

Melanie was a distraction, though, and so Zane put her out of his mind and concentrated on his mission.

Deep in the mountains, hidden by trees and on a road that was so overgrown he hardly got his bike up it, Eldric waited for him. Zane noted the three other vampires with him, but didn't allow that to throw him off. Relief washed over him when he saw his mother. She was a little paler than normal, but her hands were clenched, her jaw tight and fire in her eyes. There were no injuries that Zane could see.

"You're here earlier than I expected," Eldric noted, cocking his head to one side. "Were you planning on going right to the entrance to the kingdom? If my men hadn't seen you, you might have been torn apart by vampires not part of my little scheme."

"Scheme is right." Zane stalked over to them and thrust the money at Eldric before focusing on his mother. "Are you okay?"

She nodded.

Eldric snorted, rolling his eyes, and counted the money. A pleased smile spread over his face and he handed the bags to one of his men, who took off through the forest. Sunlight glinted off his elongated fangs. Thunder's nostrils flared. He wished he could just kill the son of a bitch.

"What do you even want that money for?"

Eldric considered him for a moment as Zane put a protective arm around his mother. The vampire's gaze flickered to her for a brief second, and Zane nearly stepped back and took the question back. He had just handed over a good chunk of money, though, and he thought that he deserved to know what it was going to be used for.

"I'm buying a yacht," Eldric said eventually. "I'm going to sail across the ocean for a hundred years, drinking champagne and fucking beautiful women."

Zane snorted in disbelief.

"I have been confined to darkness for over a thousand years, boy. I want to have fun again. No more limitations, just me and the sun and all the women I want..." Eldric smiled. "After all, what's the point of being able to go out in sunlight if I just continue to live in a dark, moldy mountain?"

"And how can you walk in sunlight now?"

Eldric burst into laughter. "If I told you, you'd do everything you could to take it away from us again. No. That can just be a mystery, my boy. Just a mystery."

Zane's mother put a hand on his arm. "Get me out of here."

He nodded, put an arm around her and glared at the three remaining vampires. None of them moved to stop him, which only caused his wolf even more irritation. Was Eldric genuine in wanting the money and nothing more? So he could have a hundred-year party? He must have been underground for a long time if he thought that much money was going to be enough to pay for all that time.

“If you wanted to join me on my yacht, I’d be more than happy to have you,” Eldric continued, keeping pace beside him, though there was a good yard between them. “All I’d want is a little of your blood every now and then, since it tastes so good. Not as good as your father’s, though. But you are a unique bunch, aren’t you? Normally, shifter blood tastes like mud, but yours?

Bet it's even better with the endorphins in your system... I can smell that little cat all over you. Sex does make blood sweeter..."

Zane's mother shuddered, and Zane hurried her the last few steps to the bike. It wasn't ideal for her, but it was better than nothing. He couldn't have brought a car all the way up here. He would have to push their speed until they were out of vampire territory. Hopefully it wouldn't be too much for her. If it was, he'd just have to call someone to come pick them up at the base of the mountain.

"If you marry your kitten," Eldric continued, talking faster now, "you'll have to invite me to your wedding. After all, we are deeply connected. I've been looking out for you all these years.

Besides, I can bring a lot to the marriage bed. Just ask your mother."

Zane knew that Eldric was trying to goad him, but that last phrase made his head whip around. His wolf snarled, and he bared his teeth. The vampire grinned at him, sticking his hands in his pockets and rocking back on his heels.

"Zane," his mother pleaded, grasping the back of his jacket. "Let's go."

"But Felicia, things are just starting to get interesting." Eldric sidled forward.

The hair stood up on Zane's neck. He fought his wolf, knowing he needed to just get on the bike and drive away. He couldn't, though. Not when the vampire was looking at him like that, as though he had just struck gold.

“Didn’t your mother ever tell you about us, boy?” Eldric smiled. “If it wasn’t for the Brotherhood’s interference, you would have grown up with me as your daddy… Funny, isn’t it? Dear Felicia had two men on her wedding night, and now she’s alone. All she’s got is a son who killed both her husbands. Maybe I should give her a third husband, eh?”

His wolf howled, the sound bursting from his throat. He wouldn't believe those lies, but the rage rose up in him, stronger than anything he’d felt before. He lunged for Eldric. His mother let out a cry. Before he reached the vampire, the two cronies darted between them. Zane punched one in the face and it stumbled back, hissing between its teeth. The other swiped at him with a knife, but he ducked.

Eldric's laughter grew louder.

With a shout, Zane launched himself at one of the vampires. He got it in a headlock and punched hard into the ribs. He felt bone snapping and dropped it. They might be undead, but they weren't immune to pain. The vampire whimpered and writhed.

The other crony got to its feet, but Zane's eyes were locked on Eldric. He held a cellphone in his hand. A thrill of fear went through him and he lunged, pulling a stake from his belt as he did so. He swung, aiming for Eldric's chest. A scream rent the air and the other vampire threw itself between them. The stake plunged into its chest, driving to its heart.

The vampire burst into ash, piling on the ground.

Zane charged for Eldric again, but he didn't reach him. His feet were suddenly kicked out from under him. Two more vampires charged out of the trees and tackled him. His arm was yanked behind his back, the stake ripped away from him. Heavy boots collided with his back, forcing him face-down into the dirt. His heart hammered as he struggled against the iron grips. There were at least four of them now; had they been in the bushes, waiting for him to kill someone?

He was flipped over to stare up at Eldric, who smiled at him. Somewhere, Zane heard his mother calling for him, but it seemed very, very far away. He twisted desperately to see she was no longer on the bike.

"Thank you, my boy." Eldric knelt beside him and patted his cheek. "You've just earned me a free kill. I know exactly who I'm going to choose, too."

Zane snarled, fighting to free himself. "Stay away from my mother!"

A smile spread over Eldric's face and he tisked. "Oh, Zane, my boy. I'm not interested in a frail old body like hers. She was beautiful forty years ago, but now? Now she's far too breakable. I like my partners able to keep up with me. No. You'll find out who it is soon enough." The vampire got to his feet and turned to the cronies. "Let him go after I'm gone. And remember, Zane, for every vampire you kill, I get to kill a shifter. And I know the names of all your friends."

"My mother!" Zane shouted, freeing one hand and punching a vampire in the face.

“I’m having her taken home, Zane. Don’t worry. When you get back, you’ll find her in perfect condition.”

Eldric smiled and walked away. A twig cracked under his heel and Zane’s eyes widened. Vampires, even when they appeared to be walking, hovered just over the ground. They never left behind footprints, let alone breaking twigs. Was that connected to their ability to walk in the sunlight? Whatever they did, what if it made them more human?

“Don’t know why we can’t just kill him,” one of the vampires grumbled. “Damn animal.”

“Oh, he’ll be dead soon enough.” Another of the vampires leered at him. “Eldric’s smart enough not to choose this one to pay for the death because that king of theirs, Typhoon, he's gonna kill this wolfy for the trouble he caused. Isn't that right, wolfy?"

Zane glared at him, but it was true. No matter how this ended, he was dead for sure. Unless he ran... That was a coward's way out, but if it meant he could ensure his mother was safe, he'd be a coward.

Melanie flashed across his mind. Would she want to be with a coward?

"Let 'im go," one of the cronies said, yawning. "You won't cause more trouble, will you?"

The vampires, grumbling, released him. Zane sprang to his feet, glaring at them. His wolf urged him to simply kill them all, but he couldn't do that. Not without sacrificing more lives. With a growl, he turned on his heel and marched for his bike.

***

As soon as he got home and saw his mother was alright, he hugged her tight. And then he grabbed a bag and started stuffing clothes into it.

"I'm taking you to Hurricane's." The vampires might still be a threat and they might not be. In any case, Hurricane would be far better able to protect her than leaving her alone in this house. "Is there anything particular you need?"

"Zane." His mother sank into the couch, wiping her face with her trembling hand. "Sit down and talk."

He knew what she wanted to talk to him about and he shook his head. There wasn't time to waste on Eldric's lies. He had been hoping to provoke Zane into an attack, and he had unfortunately succeeded. That didn't mean that Zane was going to agonize over it; no, the best thing to do now was ignore what the vampire had said and focus on what needed to be done.

"It was true," his mother said softly.

Bile churned in his stomach. "No."

"Before you were born, before we even knew he was a vampire, your father and I... Eldric was our lover."

A shudder ran down Zane's spine and he spun on his heel. His wolf growled. "No!"

His mother looked so old, so fragile. She sagged into the couch, the cushions nearly swallowing her. Her head bowed to her chest. Zane's blood was cold as he stared at her, unable to speak. It was impossible. Eldric must be threatening her or… or… He suddenly remembered the way she flinched every time Eldric called him 'my boy'. His increased immunity to vampire venom…

Zane shook as his wolf retreated, whimpering.

"When we met him, he was all charm and grace. Neither of us ever considered anything but monogamy, but somehow Eldric changed our minds. Shortly after, we began feeling off… there were strange scabs on our bodies and we didn't know what they were from. He was siphoning off our blood while we slept. Then the Brotherhood came, and we found out what he was… he tried to kill your father and take me as his prisoner."

Zane slowly moved to the couch and sank down next to his mother.

"He's obsessed with the idea of creating a new breed of vampire-shifter hybrids. He thinks that if he fathers a new breed, he will end up a god on earth."

It was all too much, but Zane had to know. His hands shook, and his stomach turned, but he forced himself to meet his mother's eyes. "Did he succeed?"

"Zane..."

"Is he my father?" his voice was little more than a whisper.

His mother looked away. "If it's possible for vampires to have children, then it's possible. I don't know for certain."

Zane leaned forward, hiding his face in his hands. That was the last thing he expected to hear. His gut still churned, and his mind ran in circles. It was impossible, wasn't it? "I can't deal with this right now," he whispered. "I'm taking you to Hurricane, Ma. Where you'll be safe."

## Chapter Nine

*Melanie*

Melanie woke up feeling like she had slept for a week. Every muscle in her body had a pleasant sort of tingling in it, even though she ached a little. As she lay in bed, smelling Zane on the blankets and her body, she waited. For some sense of shame, some sense of having made a huge mistake, as she had always been warned. All that she felt was warmth flowing throughout her body.

She yawned, stretched, and rolled over. The cellphone Hurricane had given her sat on her nightstand, and she picked it up to find a slew of texts from Ava. Melanie's heart jumped as she opened them, dreading the worst. It wasn't anything about her father, though; instead, it was a series of texts about how Jackson and Val had sniffed out the wolf and bear that had kidnapped her. They were currently sitting in jail, and it was expected that they'd stay there for a while.

The news allowed her to breathe out a sigh of relief, happy to know that they weren't on the streets anymore. She was certain that if they were allowed to run loose, she wasn't the only one that would end up seeing them taking out a vampire due to their carelessness.

What would Ava say if she knew what had gone down between Melanie and Zane? Melanie couldn't stop a grin as she phoned her. It was going to be a shock, if she told Ava. After all, Melanie was the one who had warned Ava away from the gang in the first place. Now she had slept with one of its alphas? She chewed her lip as she rolled over, waiting for Ava to pick up.

"Melanie," Ava greeted happily. "I was wondering when you were going to call."

"I just woke up," Melanie told her. "Zane woke up, so I finally could go to bed. How's my dad?"

"He's fine. He's been telling me all about how he used to take you camping. Oh, and Lindsey stopped by, asking where you are. You haven't phoned the cafe yet?"

Melanie scowled at the mention of the cafe. She'd been gone for over a week now, and her voicemail was full of angry messages from Lindsey, the owner of the cafe, and Rodger. Neither of them seemed worried about her, just angry that she wasn't there. It made her want to simply quit them both. Move to a new city and deal with whatever came next in her own way.

"I saw that you caught those idiots who kidnapped me," Melanie said, changing the subject. "I'm glad. Although, I'm surprised that Jackson put them in jail. I thought he'd kill them."

"No." Ava sounded very self-satisfied. "I figured that you wouldn't want people to die over you, so I convinced him to just put them in jail if they turned themselves over. So, they came to the house to confess to me and plead for me to intervene on their behalf. I tell you, I was tempted to let him kill them... but like I said, I didn't think you'd want people to die for you."

Melanie nodded slowly. "Yeah. You're right about that."

Ava wasn't part of the gang, not technically. And yet, she was still mated to the alpha of the Coalfell chapter. That had nearly destroyed their friendship. The only reason Melanie hadn't pulled away entirely was because she had been afraid that Jackson would end up hurting her and their daughter. But he was completely devoted to her, and Ava was the alpha's mate.

"How... how do you stand it?"

"What?"

"The gang. Everything they do... I mean, vampires aside, they still deal drugs and rob people and all that stuff. How can you accept all the bad that they do?"

Ava was silent for a moment before she let out a sigh. “It’s hard. I have to constantly remind myself that it’s not all crime. But the thing is, if it wasn’t the Brotherhood, it’d be someone else. Jackson doesn’t allow sex trafficking or tricking people into getting into drugs. I don’t like that he’s into dealing drugs at all, but you saw what happened with that recent batch of tainted stuff. People are always going to get their drugs from somewhere. Jackson at least ensures that it’s pure and has stuff like clean needle sites set up. So people don’t accidentally kill themselves.”

“I suppose. It’s just... it’s against everything I have always thought was right...”

Ava made a soft noise of agreement. “Where is all this coming from, Mel?”

Melanie chewed her lip. Heat swirled inside of her as she pressed her face into the pillow and smelled Zane’s scent once again. “Ava, I am going to tell you something and I need you to not freak out, okay?”

“Okay…”

“Well… after Zane woke up… The woman here, Roxy, she came to his room and started stripping, saying that he needed sex to get over the venom.”

“Oh, that? Yeah, it helps some people. Vampire venom brings out base instincts, you see, and while it tends more toward the violent side of things, the desire to mate can also be really—”

Melanie huffed, cutting her off. "Shut up and listen to me, will you?"

Ava giggled and was quiet.

"Well, he turned her down. Said he was going to take care of it himself. But then he came to my room. And... well, one thing led to another and I'm not a virgin anymore." Melanie said the last bit in a rush, swinging out of bed to find her clothes. Her face burned uncomfortably even as a smile spread over it.

"Wait." Ava sounded panicked. "Wait, wait, wait. Did you sleep with him or did he...?"

It took Melanie a moment to understand what she was saying. She pulled in a sharp breath as she yanked her pants on. "I slept with him. He decided he wanted me and I wanted him, so I slept with him. It's only a one-time thing, but it was still fun."

"Oh, Mel..." Ava sighed. "How do you feel?"

"Amazing, actually. I never thought my first time would be a one-night stand, but listen to this. I, you know, finished, like a dozen times. I forgot my own name in there. It was amazing, Ava. Really, it was probably the most amazing—"

The door opened. A pale woman with blood-red eyes and fangs in her smile stood in the doorway. She grinned, her pale skin gleaming in the light. The scent of rotten fruit assaulted Melanie's nose and she let out a soft gasp, stepping backward. She wasn't fast enough, though, as the vampire charged in. The vampire grabbed her phone and smashed it before seizing her around the waist and dragging her from the room.

“Hey!” Melanie threw her head forward. Her forehead collided with the vampire’s nose. The vampire squealed, and her grip loosened just enough for Melanie to slip away. She shifted into her cat form, the clothes she’d managed to put on melting off her body. She darted for the staircase.

A pained howl came from the first floor. Melanie sprang down the stairs, aware of the vampire on her tail. When she rounded the steps and darted into the hallway, she skidded to a stop. Hurricane, half-shifted into his wolf form, was on the ground. Three dead vampires lay on the floor, their throats ripped out. A dozen more surrounded him, kicking and beating on him.

The vampire chasing her swooped down and seized her by the neck. With a cry of triumph, she hoisted Melanie into the air.

"Stop," a voice rang out.

Melanie twisted, her claws half-unsheathed, as a man strode into the hall. He frowned at Hurricane as he growled. The wolf tried to get up, but one of the vampires slammed a boot into his spine and pinned him down. The new vampire snarled and pushed the other away.

"You idiot," he snarled. "Don't kill him. I get one shifter in exchange for the man Zane killed. One. I'm not going to waste it on this wolf. He's meaningless to me… Besides, look at the mark on his neck. Someone else has claimed him."

Hurricane growled and started back up, but fell with a pained whimper.

"Stay down, boy, or else I'll have to arrange more deaths to get what I want."

Hurricane surged to his feet, howling, and the vampire punched him hard in his stomach, then headbutted him. This time when Hurricane went down, he stayed down.

The vampire shook his head. "Someone feed him your blood so he doesn't die."

The order was met with scowls, but the leader didn't care. He strode to the vampire holding Melanie and smirked. His eyes seemed to literally glow as he looked at her. When he snapped his fingers, another vampire stepped over, holding a cage made of thick steel bars. The one holding

Melanie stuffed her into it. Melanie tried to turn and scratch her, but they were too fast. The cage shut with a distinctive click.

"I am pleased to finally meet you," the leader said, smirking at her. "I'm Eldric. And you are the little kitty whose scent was all over Zane's home. He must like you a lot to introduce you to his mother. Judging by the scent at his home, you were there every day... Things must be very serious between you two."

Melanie puffed up her fur and hissed at the vampire even as her mind whirled. Clearly this guy had no clue what was really going on. If she was in her human form, she might have considered correcting him. But her first priority was to get out. Eldric said that the shifters owed him a death—and by the way he was looking at her, she knew who he had picked for his sacrifice.

Eldric hummed, taking the cage almost gingerly. He smiled once more at her, and then headed out of the mansion. Melanie yowled and hissed, trying to claw him through the bars, but it was useless. Everything she could reach was heavily protected by layers of leather. The vampire didn't even seem to notice her attempts as he carried her to a sedan and placed the cage inside before he climbed in after her.

"Oh, don't be like that," he said when she hissed again. "You are part of a research project that has been going on for almost two thousand years. Thanks to your contribution, and the contribution of other subjects like you, I am going to find a cure for vampirism."

Melanie's snarls died in her throat. She blinked, confused.

“Didn’t expect that, did you?” Eldric chuckled. “Before I was turned into a vampire—very much against my will, mind you—I was a wealthy man’s son. A learned man, I was. I took my education very seriously. I learned every science. That is perhaps the greatest thing being a vampire gave me, the ability to continue my studies and learn more about science every year. But it took almost everything away from me… even the sun.”

Melanie winced. She hadn’t thought of that. What must it be like, for a vampire? Turned against their will, their humanity stripped away. Who were they, really? The same person they were as humans, or something else? A monster, or a victim?

“I’m getting it back,” he said softly as a driver got into the car and pulled them away from the mansion. “I’ve found out how to give myself the sun back. In the end it was simple. Inject a shifter with pure venom, and then siphon their blood into a vampire’s body. Doesn’t work to drink it, but putting it directly in the vein? The process makes us more human. Takes away some of our abilities. But we have the sun back.”

Melanie watched as he closed his eyes and sighed. She slipped a paw between the bars and started to bat at the latch holding it shut. Whatever sympathy she had for him, it didn’t change the fact that he was going to kill or experiment on her or both. She had to get out of here.

“Shifters are key,” he murmured, more to himself than to her. “I’m certain of it. If I can just make a vampire-shifter hybrid. Then drinking their blood… Infusing it with our venom. I’m certain it will allow vampiric strength and longevity while allowing us almost human lives… better than human. The best of all three, without the limitations of any of them.

The latch flipped. Melanie felt a surge of triumph as the cage door swung open. Eldric’s eyes opened as she sprang out, aiming her claws at his face. The vampire let out a surprised shout as he grabbed at her. Her claws tore through his skin, releasing more of that rotten fruit scent.

The crack of a gunshot made them both jump. The car swerved, throwing Melanie to the other side of the backseat. She sprang up again and looked out the black window—her heart leapt to see Zane barreling after them, a gun in his hand. He fired again, and the back window shattered.

Eldric cursed. "Here we go again."

## Chapter Ten

*Thunder*

Eldric ducked down out of sight and Zane cursed. Not much would kill a vampire, but putting a bullet in his head would certainly slow him down. With Eldric out of view now, he took aim at the tires. He held the bike steady with one hand, took a deep breath, and squeezed the trigger. The tire blew out, making the car swerve from side to side. Zane grinned as the brakes squealed and it ran into a telephone pole.

He zipped up to the front first. The driver started to get out of the car, but Zane put a bullet in his brain. Eldric tripped out of the back. Their gazes met for a moment. Blood trickled down Eldric's face from long scratches around his eyes. Zane lifted the gun and fired.

The shot went wide. Eldric flinched, snarled, and ran. Zane whipped the bike around. He opened the gas and raced around the back of the car to the sidewalk. There, he stopped for a steadier aim and lifted the gun again. Eldric glanced back, cursed, and threw himself to the side as Zane fired again and again. His gun clicked, and he snarled, about to take off after him, when there was a meaty thud from behind him.

"Zane!"

He turned at Melanie's voice. She scrambled up from where she had fallen onto the sidewalk and stepped toward him, lifting her arms as though to embrace him. Her knees and palms were scraped, her body naked. A small cut on her lip dribbled blood.

For a fraction of a second, Zane was tempted to turn. To leave her and go after Eldric, the need for answers and revenge burning through him. But his wolf snarled and snapped at him for even daring to think such a thing. He cursed bitterly under his breath as he turned back to Eldric's fleeing form—there were other vampires and he had no idea if they were watching and would kill Melanie if he left her.

She had frozen when he swore, eyes wide.

"Get on," he told her. "Quickly, before the cops come to arrest you."

Her arms dropped, and her cheeks flushed. "Me? You're the one with the gun."

"Indecent exposure, lady. You're naked." Naked. His wolf growled again as he considered what Eldric might have done. He shrugged off his leather jacket and handed it to her. She pulled it on, huffing with apparent disgust when she tried to zip it only to find it wouldn't close over her breasts.

"Get on," Zane repeated.

Melanie climbed on behind him. The knot in his chest eased once her arms were wrapped around him, but he didn't speak. He turned the bike and took off down the road. They made it back to Hurricane's place quickly, and Zane ushered her inside. She still smelled overpoweringly like him.

"Are you okay?" he asked once they were in the hall and safe from stranger's eyes.

Melanie stared up at him. "Yeah. Sorry I stopped you from—"

"You didn't stop me." He touched the cut on her lip, eyes darkening when she winced. "You'd tell me if he hurt you, right?"

"Yeah," she breathed, eyes wide as she shuffled a little closer. "But he didn't. I got his face pretty good, though, didn't I?"

His wolf stopped its pacing. It snorted, pleased, and he couldn't stop himself from smiling. His lips tingled with the desire to kiss her. He would have, too, if she hadn't continued.

"How did you even know to come after me?"

Zane's gaze darkened slightly. "I brought Ma here, saw the vamps. Between me and Hurricane, we killed them, and then you weren't here. Grabbed one of his bikes and went after you. I knew Eldric would be heading for Easthallow, cause that's where Typhoon lives and the vamp would need his permission to claim you. I'm just glad I found you. If anything happened to you..."

He let himself trail off. His hand shook, thinking of what would have happened if he had been too late. His wolf growled with the need to protect her and he couldn't stop himself. He wrapped his arms around her and pulled her tight against him, needing to feel her in his arms. Needing her to be there and safe.

Relief washed over him. She was here. She was safe. The vamps were gone, for now. He'd need to secure the grounds, but right now all he cared about was holding her in his arms. Melanie's arms wrapped around his waist. Her face pressed into his shoulder.

"Me, too," she whispered.

Zane let out a strangled laugh. "I thought you said you didn't do gangsters."

"You said you didn't do forever."

"I wish I could tell you that I didn't and that you didn't change that." He held her tighter. "Hell, I'm screwed. I want you, Melanie. I want to do forever with you. But I can't give up my position. I can't give up the Brotherhood. And that includes everything that goes with it. I'm no knight in shining armor."

Melanie squeezed him tighter for a moment, then released him. She stepped back, her expression disappointed. "I know you can't."

There was nothing more to say. They stared at each other for a moment, and then they moved past one another, each with their own tasks to accomplish. Zane's heart sat somewhere around his toes. He had thought that Tornado and Shadow were insane for taking mates, but now he knew what it really was—not a choice. He hadn't wanted to fall in love with Melanie, but here he was. She was the center of his world and he knew he would never be allowed to keep her.

***

Typhoon arrived at the mansion looking fit to kill. Zane's own wolf rose up in answer to the threat, but when Typhoon stared at him, fury and fire in his eyes, Zane's wolf bowed to the alpha. That probably saved his life.

"Explain," Typhoon snarled at him.

Zane did, keeping his voice strong and calm. Typhoon listened, not interrupting. When he was done, Typhoon shook his head and ran a hand over his buzzed hair.

"Fucking idiot," he spat at Zane. "This is the sort of thing I need to know before it blows up into a catastrophe. Now Eldric's gone to the kings and got them breathing down my neck to allow him his kill. And if he decides to kill you, it will serve you right! Idiot! I ought to strip you of your position right now. What sort of an alpha goes fucking around like that and makes this big of a mistake? You're an idiot and I ought to tear your head off myself!"

“Hey!” A streak of brown crossed in front of him and Melanie pushed herself between the two of them. She put a hand on her hip and poked Typhoon in the chest. “You can’t talk to him like that. Who the hell do you think you are? This is the alpha you’re talking to.”

“Melanie—”

Typhoon narrowed his eyes. “He’s the alpha of the Ivywood chapter. I’m the alpha of the whole fucking Brotherhood. And who the hell are you?”

Melanie shrank back, but straightened quickly enough. “Someone who isn’t going to cringe from your big scary intimidation tactics.”

Typhoon snarled at her. Zane acted without thinking. He grabbed Melanie's arm and pulled her away from Typhoon, then planted himself in front of her. A snarl ripped from his own throat as his hackles rose. Claws started to form at the end of his fingers. Typhoon growled, but this time he didn't back down.

"Are you challenging me, Thunder?" Typhoon seemed to grow larger with every word.

"Only if you try to put your hands on my mate again."

Melanie gasped from behind him. "What the fuck?"

Zane flinched as he glanced over his shoulder. "Yeah. You're my mate. I don't like it any more than you do, but it's true. You are my mate and I won't let anyone hurt you."

"All my alphas are turning into idiots." Typhoon shook his head, looking seriously pissed off. “How long have you known that girl? A couple weeks at best? I know how you met her,” he added as Zane opened his mouth. “Shit. I ought to make it a rule that mated males are immediately cast from the Brotherhood. You realize how stupid you end up when you’re tied to a woman, especially one that has no fucking clue what the hard decisions actually mean?”

Zane stared at him for a long moment. It was what he himself had thought—and perhaps a part of him still thought it. But he couldn’t change how he felt.

Melanie pushed between them again. “Look, Typhoon or whatever your name is. You can have your temper tantrum later.”

Was she trying to get herself killed? Zane tensed as Typhoon's eyes flashed.

"Eldric wants me. But not to kill me. This whole exchange thing you've got going on? I'm damn certain that he's been stealing shifters marked for death and experimenting on them. He's using shifter blood to allow the vampires to walk around in sunlight. And he wants to make a shifter-vampire hybrid. The way he was talking, he thinks it'll make him invincible."

Typhoon's eyes grew even stormier. Zane pulled Melanie back again, ready to attack the other alpha if necessary. Typhoon didn't make any motion as though he was going to attack, though. He turned away, hands clenching and unclenching. After a long moment, he turned back to them. All emotion had been completely wiped from his face.

"I'll look into that. If there are shifters being held in the vampire kingdoms, then the vamps will pay. But," he glared at Zane again, "that doesn't change the fact that you killed a vampire in vampire territory. By the treaty, a life must be given in exchange for that life."

"You can't be serious!" Melanie lunged, and Zane caught her. Her green eyes glowed and sharp claws formed at her fingertips. "Eldric attacked first! He bit Zane, he drank his blood and kidnapped his mother! Doesn't that break your little treaty? Or does that not matter, you're still going to hand me over to them?"

Typhoon shook his head, allowing Zane to relax. “Eldric has no claim to you. Under the old contract they could choose their sacrifice at will, but under the new terms, the life given is the one who killed the vamp in the first place.”

Zane nodded, grim. He would accept that if it meant Melanie was safe.

She, however, began to curse up a storm, shouting and spitting while her teeth sharpened. Zane, fearing that she would attack Typhoon and get herself hurt, wrapped his arms around her waist and dragged her away from him. He pinned her elbows to her sides, but she thrashed, writhed and spat continually.

“You know the history between me and Eldric. He targeted me on purpose, goaded me—”

“We all know the history between you,” Typhoon interrupted. “And Eldric himself slipped up and mentioned drinking from you in Brotherhood territory. Using that, I was able to negotiate. The two of you will fight to the death at the next full moon. And that’s the best I can do for you.”

Zane relaxed. He was bigger and stronger than Eldric, he stood a good chance in a one-on-one fight. The vampire kings must have agreed to it because they were tired of Eldric’s dramatics, too.

It was a mistake to loosen his grip though, because as soon as he did, Melanie tore herself away. Her fist flew, smacking Typhoon right in the nose. His head jerked back, and he let out an odd huff. Zane cursed, grabbed her and spun around so whatever retaliation Typhoon would have would go on him rather than her.

"Your rules suck," Melanie howled. "They suck big time!"

Typhoon rubbed his nose, checked his hand for blood, and glared at her. "Keep your fuzzy little tail out of Brotherhood business."

"I'm Zane's mate," she shot back, struggling against his hold. "That means Brotherhood business is my business!"

Typhoon growled and pointed a finger at her, but he addressed Zane. "Get that cat out of my sight before I snap her neck."

Zane snarled, his wolf bristling at the threat to his mate, but he was smarter than to try to fight this one out. He seized Melanie around the waist and threw her over his shoulder. While she kicked and screamed at him to put her down, he raced away. He didn't stop until they were in her bedroom and he'd shut the door. It was only there that he put her down.

Tears rolled down her face. "Eldric is the one who attacked you, he ought to be the one in the noose."

"I'm going to be fine. He's scrawny and always runs when there's a fight." Zane wrapped his arms around her gently. "Don't worry about me."

"Of course I'm going to worry about you. You're my mate."

Zane flinched, stepping back.

Melanie's eyes widened. She turned her gaze away. "Oh. You were just saying that."

"No..." Zane took her hand and led her to the bed, uncertain how to continue this. "Um... Melanie... about what Eldric said about vampire-shifter hybrids..."

She shrugged, not looking at him still. "What about it?"

Zane swallowed hard. "I... I might be one."

"*What*?"

"Not so loud," Zane hissed. He glared at her for a moment, but she just glared right back. "There is a possibility that Eldric is my father. But nobody can know."

Melanie opened her mouth, then closed it again. Clearly too stunned to speak.

Mirthless laughter bubbled up Zane's throat. "I've spent half my life fighting vampires. Now it turns out I might be the enemy I've always fought. But it makes sense. Vampire venom... it affects me differently. I have a high resistance and even when I'm in the rabid stage, I don't lose my mind...not usually, at least. God! If I'm one of them—"

"It doesn't change you."

Zane was silent.

"If Eldric fathered you, that means he's always been the one that fathered you. It doesn't change who you are, Zane." She cupped his face in her hands and pressed a soft kiss to his mouth. "It doesn't change the way I feel, or what you mean to me. You are my mate. I didn't realize it until you said it, but it's the only thing that makes sense. You're my mate and I love you."

Tears burned his eyes. Zane wrapped his arms around his mate, taking comfort in her presence. His mouth pressed to hers and they hungrily tore at each other, desperate to be close, to have this moment while the world faded away around them.

# Chapter Eleven

*Melanie*

Melanie dressed slowly the next morning, wanting to avoid leaving the bedroom with Zane for as long as possible. He, on the other hand, dressed fast. Once he was done, he lounged on the bed and watched her, a small smile on his face. Anxiety sat like a twisting ball in her stomach, making it difficult to concentrate on anything else.

"The full moon isn't for another few days," he told her. "And I have time to train. I'll be fine."

She glanced over at him. "When are you going to tell your mother?"

Zane turned his face away and shook his head. "I'm not. The stress..."

And what if Eldric killed him? She didn't say it out loud. If she pretended like there was no chance of that, then perhaps there wasn't. Zane was strong. He was big, and fast, and a skilled fighter. Eldric was thin, like a little stick.

But every time they'd faced off already, he had been weakened by the blood transfer that allowed him to be in the sunlight. When he and Zane fought this time, it would be at night. The vampire would be at full strength. Being a vampire meant that he was a lot stronger than he looked, too. No shifting would be allowed, which meant that Zane would be weakened, having to stay in his human form.

*That's what the training is for,* she reminded herself. *Because he needs to be at top fighting form, and we are going to make sure he is.*

Zane wrapped his arms around her and pulled her back against him. He nibbled at her neck. “I’ll be fine. But I do need to get busy training. Okay?”

Reluctantly, she nodded. She dressed quickly after that and went to the training room. They passed Hurricane on the way there and he gave them a distracted smile. His arm was heavily bandaged, and he walked with a slight limp. He didn’t say anything, though.

Four men waited for them in the training room. Zane introduced three of them to her as Kai, Carl, and Tom. The fourth was Typhoon. She scowled at him as he roughly greeted Zane and ignored her. Zane was tense himself, nodding stiffly at Typhoon before he murmured something to Tom and climbed into the fighting ring. Tom came to stand next to her, a grin on his face.

"So, you're Thunder's mate, are you?" He winked at her. "Lucky girl."

"Yeah. I am." She wrapped her arms around her waist and focused on the fight.

Her nerves thrummed as Zane and Typhoon faced off with each other. Carl called for the fight to start—and before Melanie even saw Typhoon move, Zane was on the mats. She gasped, clapping both hands to her mouth. Zane glanced at her, a worried look on his face, and Typhoon punched him across the face. Blood burst into the air.

"No fair!" Melanie screamed, starting forward, but Tom caught her and held her back. "He was distracted."

Typhoon glared at her. "You don't think he'll be distracted during the fight? That he won't get beaten and bloody and that when you scream he'll look at you?" He helped Zane back to his feet. "When you're facing off with Eldric, if you take your eyes off him for a second, you're dead."

Zane grunted, but nodded. Carl called for the second round to begin. This time, Melanie worked on keeping her emotional outbursts to herself. Even though she whimpered or grunted with sympathetic pain every time Typhoon caught him, she forced herself not to distract Zane any more than he already was.

It didn't do much good, though. As the training wore on, for hours and hours, it was clear Typhoon was on top the whole time. By the time he called for an end, Zane was bloody and bruised, and Typhoon was hardly even sweating. Melanie had bit her tongue so hard she was bleeding and when Typhoon climbed out of the ring, she rushed past him to go to Zane.

“Take care of your mate,” Typhoon threw over his shoulder, though she wasn’t certain if he was talking to her or Zane. “Tomorrow Zane fights against Kai. You’re smaller and lighter than him. He needs to be prepared for speed as well as strength.”

He walked out without another word. Melanie took the first aid kit handed to her by Tom. Her hands trembled as she started to clean Zane up.

A week passed in much the same way. Against Tom and Carl, there was no contest. Zane came out on top every time. With Kai, it was far more evenly matched. But against Typhoon, there was no contest. Melanie tended to his injuries after the fights and stayed with him every day. Typhoon forbade Zane from training for two days before the fight, so that he could be fully healed from his injuries.

And then it was the full moon.

The fight was taking place in a large field, with a ring of trees around the edge. The field had been torn up and flattened, then compressed so that it was hard, flat dirt that the two would be fighting on. Melanie stood with Zane, her stomach tying itself into knots as Typhoon bound Zane's knuckles and gave him a few last-minute pointers. In the lines of indifference on his face,

Melanie thought she caught a look of concern.

Just as they were finishing up, a vampire came striding toward them. He was the most muscular of the vamps and had a scowl on his face.

“Cromwell,” Typhoon snarled. “Is your man backing out?”

“No. But he is insisting that he have a private word with Thunder, Melanie and yourself.”

Melanie frowned. What did he want? She glanced at the two men, and both scowled. Zane looked about ready to say no way, but Typhoon gave him a hard look and nodded. Cromwell snorted and they all headed across the field, to where a small tent had been erected for the vampires. Eldric waited for them inside the tent. He was shirtless and wore a pair of loose shorts. He was more muscular than Melanie had given him credit for, but still nothing compared to Zane. That helped ease her fears a little, but when he grinned at her, her stomach clenched again.

“Ah, good, good. I was hoping that you would come.” Eldric smiled at them. “I was hoping that we could make this little fight more entertaining. Higher stakes and all that.”

“Not interested,” Typhoon said.

Eldric gave him a disgusted glance. “I wasn’t talking to you, was I? No. Zane. My boy. If this is going to be the day one of us dies, then I want it to be well worth it. So, in that case, I propose that if you win, your father’s remains are returned to you.”

Zane's breath hitched, and Melanie took his hand.

"And if I win, then Melanie belongs to me. Since someone went and gave away my other subjects." Here, Eldric glared at Cromwell, who looked nonplussed.

Even before Zane growled, Melanie knew what his answer was going to be. And she knew, deep in her heart, that she had to stop him. Because if he lost, she knew Eldric would find a way to get her anyway. And if he won? Well... he had to win.

"Deal," she blurted, just as Zane said, "No deal."

Zane and Typhoon both whirled to stare at her, and she squeezed Zane's hand harder. "You're not going to lose."

Eldric chuckled. “If that’s what you want to think. Now can I have a word with my future bride alone?”

“No!” Zane yelled, but Melanie released his hand. She gave him an apologetic look. He stared at her, a growl on his lips.

Typhoon gave her a hard look, then grasped Zane’s arm and pulled him out. Cromwell looked between her and Eldric for a moment before he turned on his heel and marched out. Her cat hissed to be in such close proximity to the vampire, alone, but she folded her arms and lifted her chin, glaring at him.

“Well, what do you want?”

“To tell you that I’ve finally figured out how to make vampire-shifter hybrids and that I can’t wait to make you the mother of a new breed.”

The leer on his face was nothing compared to the looks she was used to getting at the Chubby Kitty. If he thought that it was going to frighten her off, he had another thing coming. Far from frightening her, his proclamation made a triumphant grin spread over her face. He didn't realize it, but he'd just answered a question that had haunted Zane for over a week now.

"That means you're not his father," she whispered. "All these head games you've been playing with him. And you knew that."

Eldric's eyes widened briefly, then they narrowed. "Get out, girl."

"Don't get mad at me just because you messed up," Melanie cooed, and quickly slipped away. She hurried out to where the other shifters waited. She gave Zane a grin, to which she got a puzzled look in return, and pulled him away from the tent. As Eldric came out and declared it was time for the fight, she pressed herself to her tiptoes and whispered in Zane's ear. "He's not your father. Now kill the fucking bastard."

Zane glanced at her, surprised, but a smile spread over his face. He gave her a quick kiss, and then moved to face off with Eldric. Cromwell and Typhoon both reviewed the rules, and then backed away. Melanie chewed on her thumb, watching as her stomach started to curl in around itself. Zane would win. He had to win.

Unbidden, images of when Zane fought Typhoon came to her mind. Of Zane being beaten to the ground again and again and again.

Eldric made the first move. He zipped across the space separating them and cast a punch at Zane's face. Zane sidestepped and grabbed Eldric's arm. He slammed his palm into Eldric's upper arm, causing the arm to jerk at an odd angle. Eldric let out a grunt of pain even as he whirled. His fist clipped Zane on the chin this time. Zane kicked out his feet.

The vampire used the momentum of his fall to wrap his legs around Zane's. He swept Zane off-balance and they both fell heavily. Zane flipped over, ready to attack once more. Before he could, Eldric had rolled up and elbowed him in the neck. Zane fell again and Eldric wrapped an arm around his neck.

A scream tried to work its way out of Melanie's throat. She pressed both hands over her mouth. Blood tasted in her mouth, she bit her tongue so hard.

Zane threw an elbow back, hitting Eldric square in the jaw. The vampire reeled back. His hold broke, and Zane threw him off. They both scrambled back to their feet and circled each other, looking for openings. Melanie bit down harder on her tongue. Eldric's eyes glowed and his fangs were bared. Zane panted, mouth slightly open, and he dodged in again. He seized Eldric and lifted him; it was a move he'd used against the others, throwing them down to the ground.

Only this time, Eldric grabbed his hair, yanking his head back, and sunk his fangs into Zane's mouth.

“No!” Melanie screamed. She started forward, but both Tom and Carl stopped her.

Cromwell and Typhoon were both at the fighters in a second. They both seized Eldric and dragged him back. Eldric started to laugh as Typhoon released him, leaving him to Cromwell, and rushed to Zane. Worry was clear on his face now. Zane clutched at his neck as blood ran down it. The hands holding Melanie tightened as she struggled to free herself.

“If you go in now, you’ll get hurt,” Tom whispered.

“Well, that was against the rules,” a shifter behind them muttered.

Typhoon jumped to his feet and came at Eldric and Cromwell while Zane staggered to his feet. They argued quickly for a moment before Cromwell glared at Eldric and nodded. Relief washed over Melanie, thinking that it was over, that it was an automatic forfeit on Eldric's part. But then alpha and king both moved out of the way.

"Since the shifter has been bitten, he is free to shift," Cromwell declared. "You may resume."

Before Melanie could even protest the unfairness of it, Eldric charged. He punched Zane in the face, stomach, ribs. Zane stumbled back, weakly trying to defend himself. She screamed his name and his head turned ever so slightly. Eldric went in, hands like claws. And in the blink of an eye, Zane had shifted into his huge black wolf. His teeth caught Eldric's hand.

Melanie gasped. Zane snarled, tossing Eldric over his shoulder. The vampire landed heavily and screamed as Zane came at him again. The screams cut off abruptly, but Zane didn't stop. Snarls and growls flew, accompanied by bits of Eldric. The vampires all drew back and even the shifters were afraid to get too close.

All except for Typhoon. He shifted into a wolf twice the size of Zane and bowled into him. Zane turned, snapping his teeth, but Typhoon seized him in his jaws and pinned him down. His gaze flickered to her and she knew without words what she needed to do.

"Wait!" Tom called as she raced across the field.

Melanie ignored him. She got to the two snarling wolves quickly and shifted. Though instinct told her to run, she instead maneuvered around their bodies to the bleeding wound in Zane's neck and began to lick it clean. Zane snarled, jerked and then went still. She continued to lick and clean until he had shifted back to his human form. Then she shifted as well and locked her lips around his wound, sucking out the venom.

Typhoon shifted back as well, crouched beside them with a firm hold still on Zane. "You're going to be okay, Thunder," he promised. "You're going to be okay."

## Chapter Twelve

*Thunder*

*One Month Later*

Zane undid his tie. The burning ball of anxiety and fear that had been in him every day for the past month was finally gone. He was back to full strength, having fully recovered from Eldric's underhanded tricks. His position with the Savage Brotherhood was still secure, too, Typhoon simply making him promise never to pull such a bone-headed move again before telling him he'd take no disciplinary action.

And today, finally, the prisoners that Eldric had been keeping were released, and Zane had received his father's remains. They were being kept in a morgue for now, until he and his mother could make all the arrangements to have him buried properly. Until he saw them for himself, he had been uncertain that the vampires were going to honor that deal.

Melanie wrapped her arms around his neck as the door swung shut. After the trauma at Zane's house, his mother wasn't comfortable staying there, but Hurricane had graciously allowed them to stay at his place for the time being. Zane smiled at his mate, wrapping his arms around her waist as she pressed herself to her toes to give him a small kiss.

"How are you?" she asked him.

"I'm good. Relieved." Zane smoothed her hair from her face. "And you? How are you doing?"

"I'm not the one who got his father's bones today."

Zane hummed. “But you did put your father into a nursing home.”

Melanie flinched. “I know that it’s the best for him. He needs more attention than I can give him. Just from a medical standpoint, it needed to happen. I know that. It doesn’t make me stop feeling like a failure as a daughter, though. I am grateful Hurricane gave us the money to get him into that one he wanted, though. He seems to be settling in well. Making new friends.”

It was what the doctors had recommended, but Zane knew Melanie's reluctance. The fact of the matter, though, was that her father was in much worse physical health than his mother and could hardly move himself around anymore. In the place he was in now, he was receiving more care and his caretakers were able to give him more than Melanie could, including regular trips out to various sightseeing locations.

"He'll be happier staying in Coalfell, anyway."

Melanie nodded. "I promised to visit every weekend, though."

"And I will be there at your side." Zane twined his fingers through hers and brought their hands to his mouth, so he could kiss each of her knuckles. "Because that is what a mate does."

"Mates." Melanie's face broke into a smile. She kissed him again, nibbling at his lower lip then grinning. "I like the sound of that. And to think, all these years I was saving myself for someone special… I never expected it to be my mate, though."

Zane laughed softly, turning her so he could walk her to the bed. "I never expected to find a mate. Let alone one that could accept this... crazy life of mine. Are you sure you're okay with being mated to a gangster?"

"Are you okay with being mated forever?" she shot back and winked. She grew serious quickly, though. "I love you, Zane. Being part of the Brotherhood is part of who you are. Yeah, there are things I don't like. But in the end, I have to accept them if I'm going to accept you. You do a lot of good. And without you as the alpha, the local chapter might have an alpha more like Typhoon. Bloodthirsty."

He tipped her back on the bed and took a moment for his gaze to trail over her. He felt himself swelling as she ran her hands over her own curves, tempting him with a sultry look. When she paused at her breasts and squeezed them, he nearly forgot what they were talking about.

"Uh... right. Typhoon. He's not a bad guy, really. Just lots of pressure."

"Hmm. Well, I understand why you have to do what you do."

Zane broke from his ogling to return to her face. It was open, genuine and honest. Another small ball of anxiety in his chest released. He grinned and started to unbutton his shirt, keeping her eye. He intended to let her know exactly how grateful he was to her. Melanie let out a soft moan and sat, reaching to help him. Her fingers made quick work of his buttons, and as she moved to his pants, he unzipped her dress.

"I've been thinking. I want to buy the Chubby Kitty," she said, intent on her mission. When she dropped his pants, she took him in her hand. He, on the other hand, was still working at getting her dress off.

"Why do you want to buy a strip club?"

"So Rodger isn't the owner. I want to protect those girls. They're in a vulnerable position and I... I want to make their lives better, even if it's just a little bit."

"And that's what I love about you." He started to harden in her hand, and, impatiently, pulled her to her feet. He pulled her dress over her head and tossed it to the floor. Moving quickly, he unsnapped her bra and set her breasts free. They bounced slightly as he dipped her back onto the bed. Lifting one foot and then the next, he removed the rest of her clothes and kissed his way up her leg. "I love you."

"I love you, too." Melanie tangled her hand into his hair, resting her head on one arm.

Zane loved watching the pleasure take her as he kissed up her inner thigh. He had discovered long ago that, although he didn't enjoy receiving oral sex, he certainly loved giving it. A flush rose up his mate's cheeks as he coasted from her thigh to her hip and continued his way to her navel before working his way back down the other side.

"Don't tease me," she sighed. Her beautiful body arched to him as her eyes started to flutter shut. "Not today. I want you inside of me."

Zane sighed, a little disappointed, but there was time for teasing later. He spread her thighs a little further apart and licked at her clit with his tongue. His efforts were rewarded at once. Melanie arched her back, letting out a soft moan. He continued to work at her, trailing his hands up and down her legs as her hand tightened in his hair, then relaxed to comb her fingers through it.

"I love it when you do that," she sighed.

Zane hummed, burying his face into her so he could suck on her sensitive little nub. She let out another moan, rocking her hips slowly. She really was demanding today. He laughed softly, moving back so he could insert a finger into her. She was already slick and ready, but he wasn't ready to see her pleasure end just yet.

He went back to her, until her legs were trembling, and she let out a soft cry. Her head lolled to one side as he gently let her down. A sexy smile crossed her face. Just the sight of her, combined with her heavenly scent and taste, made him harden. He kissed his way back up her body, pausing at her breasts. It was one of his favorite parts, taking the nipple into his mouth and feeling it harden under his tongue. He probed gently, while Melanie wrapped her arms around his shoulders. He kept one hand between her thighs, stroking her just enough to keep her riding high, just one edge.

Her pale skin turned a fetching shade of pink as he kept working her, kissing his way up her throat to her mouth. She eagerly kissed him, one hand roaming over his body while the other reached for him. She took care of him with firm, even strokes, making his back buckle as his hips moved with her rhythm. The kiss deepened, their tongues tangling.

"I love you," Melanie murmured again, lifting herself up to kiss at his neck, nip at his shoulder. His skin tightened, and he hardened to a point where it nearly hurt. Well, Melanie wanted fast today… he'd give her fast and then he'd give himself slow. All night slow. He buried his face in her neck, loving the way she writhed under him, the way her strokes faltered.

Zane inhaled her scent, then frowned. He pulled back slightly. "Are you using a new shampoo?"

Melanie's brows arched. "No. Why?"

“It’s just... you smell different. Just a little.” He cocked his head, trying to figure it out, then shrugged. He slid two fingers inside of her and stroked her from the inside while circling her clit with his thumb. “How does that feel?”

“Amazing.” Melanie released him to grasp both shoulders. She arched her hips up in a steady motion, panting. Her breasts bounced as she heaved. “Not as amazing as it would feel with you inside of me, though.”

“Subtle.”

Zane cut off whatever protest she might have to his teasing with a searing kiss. He grasped her thighs and knelt between them, bringing them both to his hips. Then, staring into the eyes of his mate, he entered her. They were so used to each other by now that there was no waiting needed. He began to rock his hips in an easy motion, bracing himself on his hands so he could look down at her beautiful face.

God, he was lucky. Her eyes glowed with love, her fingers warm against him as he steadily thrust into her. Warmth of love and heat of lust intermingled, building something so beautiful inside of him that he could hardly keep it in. He bit his lip, fighting against his arousal to make it as long as possible for her.

“You look so cute when you do that,” Melanie panted, then neither of them could talk.

Their bodies moved in unison, thrusting together in harmony. That heat inside of him twisted, making everything feel hot. All his muscles tensed with anticipation. Melanie's eyes rolled into the back of her head and her fingers tightened into his skin. When she let out a series of small cries and clenched around him, Zane allowed himself to let go.

Pleasure rushed over him, blinding him with wave after wave of darkness. He fell to his elbows, keeping himself up and moving through sheer force of will. When Melanie screamed again, her voice infused with passion, he dropped to one side, unable to support himself any longer. He kissed her neck again and again, grunting as he attempted to keep her pleasure.

When she started to giggle breathlessly, her fingers in his hair, he knew there was no more. He let himself still, burying his face in her neck. He breathed in her scent, loving it. As he caught that slight change again, a fierce protectiveness rose up in him.

His head jerked up as it all clicked. A laugh burst from him. “You’re pregnant,” he breathed.

Melanie stared at him for a moment. “Uh... pretty sure it takes longer than that.”

“Silly. You were pregnant already. That’s why your scent changed.”

“But... how do you know from my scent?”

Zane grinned at her, his hand trailing down to rest of her stomach, where his cub was growing. “A mate knows, my dear. A mate knows.”

*****

THE END

28058052R00153

Printed in Poland
by Amazon Fulfillment
Poland Sp. z o.o., Wrocław